D0456767

The Secret of Candlelight Inn

"Did you find anything?" Marisa asked.

Nancy tugged on a square wall panel. "Yes. I think this is some sort of hidden entrance, but I can't get it open."

Nancy knew that a lot of old houses had secret rooms and hidden passageways. She had an idea. "Joan?" she called. "Do you think you could tug on the floorboard out there?"

Joan pulled the floorboard upward. After a few inches, it made a sound like a gunshot, and the panel in the closet creaked open.

Nancy tugged the panel away from the wall and brushed away several cobwebs. She shone the flashlight through the large opening and gasped at what she saw.

Stacked neatly from floor to ceiling in the tiny room were piles and piles of money.

Nancy Drew
Mystery Stories

Available from Simon & Schuster

Keene, Carolyn.
The secret of
Candlelight Inn /
1997.
33305230624953
ca   06/24/14

NANCY DREW® 139

THE SECRET OF
CANDLELIGHT INN

CAROLYN KEENE

Aladdin Paperbacks
New York   London   Toronto   Sydney   Singapore

If you purchased this book without a cover, you should be aware that this book is stolen property. It was reported as "unsold and destroyed" to the publisher and neither the author nor the publisher has received any payment for this "stripped book."

This book is a work of fiction. Any references to historical events, real people, or real locales are used fictitiously. Other names, characters, places, and incidents are the product of the author's imagination, and any resemblance to actual events or locales or persons, living or dead, is entirely coincidental.

First Aladdin Paperbacks edition December 2002
First Minstrel edition October 1997

Copyright © 1997 Simon & Schuster, Inc.
Produced by Mega-Books, Inc.

ALADDIN PAPERBACKS
An imprint of Simon & Schuster
Children's Publishing Division
1230 Avenue of the Americas
New York, NY 10020

All rights reserved, including the right of reproduction in whole or in part in any form.

Printed in the United States of America

20 19 18 17

NANCY DREW and NANCY DREW MYSTERY STORIES are registered trademarks of Simon & Schuster, Inc.

ISBN-13: 978-0-671-00052-3
ISBN-10: 0-671-00052-7

0412 OFF

Contents

THE SECRET OF
CANDLELIGHT INN

1

Hello, Casey

"Do you think she'll like this?" Bess Marvin held up a toy hamburger and squeaked it at her cousin, George Fayne. "The package says it has authentic meat flavor."

George made a face. "If I were a dog, I think I'd rather have a steak—a *real* one."

"I have a steak in here, too." Bess leaned over and rummaged through the large canvas bag at her feet. She pulled out a plastic steak, a rubber newspaper, a rawhide shoe, a tennis ball, and a library book.

George read the book's title. "*Raising a Well-Adjusted Puppy.* Will two dozen toys make her well-adjusted?"

"I don't know. I haven't gotten past the first

1

chapter—'Choosing Your Puppy,'" Bess admitted.

"Well, read fast," their friend Nancy Drew said from the driver's seat of her blue Mustang. "I don't want any housebreaking accidents in my car."

"I also brought paper towels," Bess said. "Just in case."

Nancy rounded a curve and turned onto a road nearly hidden by leafy, golden maples. "Do you get to choose your puppy?" she asked Bess. "Or did the Guiding Eyes already assign you one?"

"They've assigned one to me—a female golden retriever named Casey." Bess sighed. "I guess I shouldn't say 'mine.'"

"I think you're doing a wonderful thing, Bess." Nancy glanced at her friend in the rearview mirror. "Caring for a puppy until she's old enough to be trained as a guide dog for the blind."

Bess twirled a strand of long, blond hair around her finger. "I hope I don't get too attached."

"How long will you have her?" George asked.

"Fifteen months," Bess replied. "Then she goes to guide dog school. If she passes, she'll become a guide to someone who is blind. But if she flunks, I'll get a chance to adopt her permanently."

Nancy inched the car up a steep incline. "Where do I turn, Bess?"

Bess peered out the window. "There's a hidden entrance, I think—wait—over there!"

Nancy hit the brakes hard, then skillfully guided the car around a hairpin turn.

"Sorry," Bess said. "I've only been to Candlelight Inn once."

"No wonder it went out of business," George said. "Nobody could ever find the place."

A few minutes later, Nancy parked the car along the side of a steep driveway lined with apple trees. Branches bent with green fruit dangled a few inches above the car's hood.

Nancy, Bess, and George crunched through fallen leaves as they climbed the hill to the old Candlelight Inn. Black shutters framed the windows of the three-story gray stone building with two crumbling brick chimneys.

Brown leaves swirled around them, and a chilling gust of wind raised goose bumps on Nancy's arms. A lacy curtain in one of the second-floor windows swayed slightly. Was someone watching them? Nancy wondered.

Bess looked at her watch. "We're a little early. The breeders aren't bringing the puppies until two o'clock."

The front door opened, and a girl whom Nancy judged to be about eight years old sprinted down the hill toward them.

"Bess!" the girl called. Her light brown pony-tail flew out behind her. "I saw you through the window. Is Casey here?"

"Not yet," Bess said. "Nancy and George, do you remember my neighbor, Amber Marshall?"

Nancy smiled at Amber. "Of course. It's nice to see you again."

"You, too." Amber jumped up and down. "I'm so excited. I can't wait to meet the puppies!"

"Bess is counting on you to help her with Casey," George said. "She's only read the first chapter of her dog-raising book."

"Don't worry, Bess. I've read three books," Amber said. "I'll help you."

"Good," Bess said, "because I'm not sure I can handle this responsibility all by myself. By the way," she added, "where's your brother?"

"He and Marisa are inside," Amber said. "Come on. Do you want a tour?"

"Sure," Bess said.

Nancy, Bess, and George followed Amber up the hill to the inn. The front door creaked loudly as Amber pushed it open. From the second floor came a pounding noise.

"Devon!" Amber called. "Bess is here."

The pounding sound stopped abruptly. Nancy squinted into the dimly lit, windowless hallway as Amber's older brother, Devon, walked down the stairs, a hammer in his hand.

4

"Devon, you remember my cousin, George, and our friend Nancy Drew," Bess said.

"Hi." Devon set down the hammer. "I'd shake your hands, but I've hammered my thumb about ten times, and it's throbbing."

"What are you working on?" Bess asked.

"I was trying to do a quick patch job on a loose floorboard." Devon rolled his eyes. "I might be able to design a building, but don't ask me to help build or fix it."

"Devon is studying architecture at Westmoor University," Bess explained to Nancy and George.

"What an interesting profession," Nancy said.

Devon shrugged. "Not really. My dad's an architect, my grandfather was an architect, so I'm going to be an architect. Either that, or I'm going to pay my own way through college."

"*I'm* going to be an architect," Amber said. "Devon's going to be an actor."

Devon smiled. "Maybe. I hope."

"Did Devon tell you he got a part in the fall play at Westmoor?" A tall brunette entered the hallway, guided by a black Labrador retriever wearing a leather harness. "He's going to play Iago in *Othello*," the woman said. She found Devon's hand and gave it a light squeeze. "We're very proud of him. Right, Amber?"

Amber nodded. "Yes, we are." She turned to

Nancy and George. "This is my brother's girl-friend, Marisa Henares. Marisa, this is Nancy and George."

Marisa smiled in Nancy and George's direction. "Pleased to meet you. I've heard so much about you from Bess."

"We've heard a lot about *you*," George said.

"Yes. We were so sorry to hear about your grandmother's death," Nancy said.

"Thank you." Marisa's dark eyes filled with tears. Sensing that she was upset, the dog began to whine and lick her hand.

Marisa cleared her throat. "Nancy and George, meet Misty. She's a black Lab, and she's the best guide dog in the world."

Amber gave Misty a hug. "See, Bess? You're going to love raising a puppy." She sighed. "I wish I could have one."

"You will—in a few more years," Devon said.

"I know, I know." Amber folded her arms across her chest. "Dad says that when I'm more mature and responsible, I can have a puppy. I bet I'll be a hundred years old before Dad thinks I'm mature and responsible. You're so lucky, Marisa."

"Before I lost my sight, I never liked dogs. Now I can't imagine living without one." Marisa patted Misty's head. "Did Devon give you the tour yet?"

"Not yet," Bess said.

"I was waiting for you," Devon told Marisa. "You're our resident expert on the history of the inn."

"Thanks for the compliment," Marisa said. "Follow us."

Marisa and Misty led the way through an arched entrance into the living room. Though the upholstery was slightly faded and worn, the large pieces of furniture were made of mahogany and looked to Nancy to be of high quality.

The room smelled musty, as if the windows had not been opened in years. Dark storm clouds had gathered outside, and the only light came from a dusty chandelier hanging from the high ceiling.

"Candlelight Inn was built in 1853 by my great-great-great-grandfather, Edward Allen Taper." Marisa ran her hand over the intricately carved wood above one of the fireplaces. "He hired the finest craftsmen in Illinois to do the construction. For more than a hundred years, the inn was the most popular place to stay in River Heights."

"Didn't I read in the newspaper that Abraham Lincoln stayed here once?" Nancy asked.

Marisa smiled. "Yes."

"Wow," Amber said. "Wait till I tell my teacher. Maybe my class can come here on a field trip."

"I'm not sure the Guiding Eyes would appreciate that," Marisa said.

Amber frowned. "Oh. I forgot."

"They'll be doing construction here for the next year or so, to convert the building into the guide dog school. The dogs will eventually be trained here, and their new owners will stay at the school for several weeks while they get acquainted with their guide dogs," Marisa explained. "When my grandmother decided to close the inn about thirty years ago, she had it remodeled to turn it into a private residence. The Guiding Eyes will have to undo a lot of the changes she made at that time."

The group made its way down the long hallway to a spacious study lined with sagging bookshelves. "This was my grandmother's favorite room," Marisa said.

"Are all these books in Braille?" Bess asked.

"Braille or large print," Marisa said. "My grandmother did have some sight until a few years ago."

"Your grandmother was blind, too?" Amber asked.

Marisa nodded. "We both had a hereditary disease called retinitis pigmentosa. I lost my sight completely when I was sixteen, but a lot of people with RP have some vision until they're much older. My mother died when she was forty-four, and she never had any vision loss. The disease skips generations sometimes."

"There sure are a lot of books here," Amber said. "I guess your grandmother liked to read."

"You're right." Marisa patted Misty's head. "How do you think she got so smart?"

"Did she really make a million dollars in the stock market?" Amber asked.

"You bet she did," Marisa said. "And she was in her seventies at the time."

"Incredible," George said.

"I'm executor of her estate, and I've been going through her paperwork. Good thing I'm taking classes in securities and taxes in law school—otherwise, I'd be very confused," Marisa said.

Amber walked over to a painting of a woman that hung over the fireplace. She read the engraved plaque on the frame. " 'Emmaline Whitby.' Who's that in the painting, Marisa?"

"That was my grandmother," Marisa said. "My mother painted that portrait many years ago. I'm told it's very good."

"It sure is," Amber said.

Bess sat down at an antique sewing machine. A raised, leafy design was carved on the surface of each of its drawers. "Someone in your family had incredible taste, Marisa. This is the most gorgeous sewing machine I've ever seen."

"You sew, don't you, Bess?" Marisa asked.

"Yes," Bess said, "although some people might disagree with me." She looked at George.

"Just because I never wear that skirt you made me . . ." George said. "It's very pretty—I just don't wear skirts. You know that."

Marisa smiled. "Would you like to have this sewing machine, Bess?"

Bess's mouth dropped open. "But—it's for the Guiding Eyes, isn't it?"

"No," Marisa said. "My grandmother left the Guiding Eyes the inn and the money to start the school. She left me all the furniture."

"Don't you want it?" Bess asked.

"Where would I put it?" Marisa asked. "I don't live here—I have a tiny apartment. Anyhow, I never learned to sew."

"But isn't the sewing machine worth a lot of money?" Bess asked.

"No," Marisa said. "This is all good furniture, but it's not especially valuable. I plan to sell most of it, but if there's anything you like, it's yours."

"I don't know what to say. This is so kind of you."

"Then you'll take the sewing machine?" Marisa asked.

"Let me check with my mother first, just to make sure we have room for it," Bess said. "Could I let you know tomorrow?"

"Of course." Marisa walked with Misty to a

desk on the other side of the room. "I think this old secretary matches it, too. And there might be a table upstairs. . . ."

Bess laughed. "I think one sewing machine will do for now, but thanks."

Amber pulled aside a heavy drape and looked out a window that overlooked the driveway. "The puppies are here!" she cried as she sprinted down the hallway and out the front door. Everyone followed her outside.

Several cars now lined the driveway, and six fluffy golden retriever puppies played with a dozen volunteer puppy-raisers in the leaves on the front lawn.

"It smells like rain," Marisa said as she drew in a deep breath.

"I hope not." Amber wrinkled her nose. "I love the dogs—except when they get wet. Yuck."

"The sun looks like it's peeking out of the clouds a little bit," Bess said hopefully.

A woman with a clipboard walked over to them. Her curly black hair was mixed with gray. "Hi, Marisa," she said.

"Hello," Marisa said. "Penny Rosen, meet Nancy Drew, George Fayne, and Bess Marvin. Penny is the coordinator of the Guiding Eyes project here in River Heights," Marisa explained. "Penny, Bess is here to pick up Casey."

Penny reached down and scooped up a puppy that had trotted over and was sniffing Misty's tail.

11

"What a coincidence," Penny said. "This is Casey. Looks like she's come to meet you."

Bess gently took the squirming dog from Penny and held her at arm's length. "You are so beautiful, Casey." Casey's chocolate-colored brown eyes and black nose stood out sharply from her light coat.

"Her hair is almost the same color as yours," Penny told Nancy.

Amber looked at Nancy's reddish blond hair. "It is. Oh, she's so pretty. May I hold her, Bess?"

"Here you go." Bess carefully passed the dog to Amber. Casey eagerly licked Amber's hand and face. Amber kissed Casey's tiny wet nose. Casey immediately jumped out of her arms and onto the lawn.

"I guess she didn't like that," Amber said.

Casey trotted over to Nancy.

"I think she just wanted to say hi to Nancy," Devon said, putting an arm around his sister.

Casey sniffed Nancy's shoe.

"Uh-oh," Amber said.

Before Nancy could move, Casey squatted and made a puddle on Nancy's shoe.

Bess gasped. "Nan! I'm sorry."

Nancy bent down and patted Casey. "I've been through much worse. Don't worry about it." She turned to Marisa. "Would you mind if I went inside to clean my shoe?"

12

"Of course not," Marisa said.

Nancy started up the hill. "I'll be right back."

Nancy took off her shoes before entering the inn. The floor felt cold through her socks. This huge place must be expensive to heat, she thought.

Nancy found some paper towels in the kitchen. In the bathroom, she turned on the old-fashioned spigot and began to clean her shoe.

Over the running water, she thought she heard the sound of a ringing telephone. She turned off the tap. Yes, it was definitely the phone. But where was it?

Dashing to the kitchen, Nancy finally found a black, wall-mounted rotary phone. The dial was labeled with Braille numbers. She picked it up. "Guiding Eyes," she said breathlessly. "May I help you?"

"Who is this?" a man's voice asked.

"My name is Nancy Drew. I—"

"Where's Marisa?" he asked.

"She's outside. Would you like to speak with her?"

"Yes, please," he said, sounding relieved. "This is Eric Pavlik—I'm a friend of hers."

"I'll get her for you," Nancy said.

Nancy raced back down the hill and found Marisa helping Bess put on Casey's collar. "Marisa, it's Eric on the phone," she said.

13

"I wonder why Eric's calling me here," Marisa said as she and Misty entered the inn with Nancy. "I hope nothing's wrong."

Nancy returned to the kitchen for her shoe and the paper towels as Marisa picked up the phone.

"Hi, Eric," Marisa said. "What's up?"

Marisa listened for a moment, then Nancy saw her face grow pale. Marisa grasped the edge of the counter, and her knuckles were white as she grasped the receiver. "You're in jail?"

2

On the Money

Marisa sank into a chair, and Misty lay down at her feet. "Okay," she said into the phone. "Tell me what happened."

Nancy decided to give Marisa some privacy. She headed back toward the bathroom with her shoe.

"Listen," she heard Marisa say, "the first thing you need to do is hire a good lawyer."

Nancy stopped. Her father was a criminal attorney—an excellent one. Maybe she should tell Marisa, in case Eric wanted to hire him.

"I'll meet you at the police station right away." Marisa hung up the phone, and Nancy returned to the kitchen.

"Oh, Nancy," Marisa said. "I guess you heard what happened."

"Sort of," Nancy said. She told Marisa about her father's experience as a criminal defense lawyer.

"Carson Drew," Marisa said. "Of course. He was a guest speaker in one of my classes. He was great."

"Would you like me to call him?" Nancy asked gently.

"That would be wonderful," Marisa said. "Eric Pavlik is one of the nicest guys in the world. You know how I met him? He/volunteered through the library as a reader for the blind. He read me all the law school assignments that weren't available on talking books or in Braille. Someone that kind is not capable of being a criminal."

"It doesn't sound like it," Nancy said. "What happened?"

"Eric was buying something at the mall. He says he was arrested for using two counterfeit twenty-dollar bills."

"I read in the paper that the police have found a lot of counterfeit money in River Heights recently," Nancy said. "What else did Eric tell you?"

"Not much, but he swore to me he's innocent. And I believe him. Eric's totally trustworthy." Marisa rubbed Misty's neck. "You like him, don't you, Misty?" Misty wagged her tail.

Nancy smiled. "Misty's a good judge of character, huh?"

16

"The best," Marisa said.

"Is it okay if I use this phone to call my father?" Nancy asked.

"Please do." Marisa and Misty stood up. "I can't thank you enough."

Nancy made her phone call and finished cleaning her shoe. She and Marisa then returned outside. Nancy saw George running up and down the hill.

"What are you doing?" Nancy asked.

"I'm in training. Penny Rosen talked me into signing up for a 5K run. One of Westmoor University's fraternities is sponsoring it to raise money for the Guiding Eyes." George slowed to a walk. "Unfortunately, the race is in two days. There's no way I'll be in peak form."

"I think the Guiding Eyes will understand," Marisa said. "You were a good sport to volunteer. And if you're taking pledges, sign me up."

"Me, too," Nancy said.

"Me, three," Bess said. She stood at the bottom of the hill with Amber, Devon, and Casey. "Not that I have a lot of money to spare after buying all those dog toys."

"Speaking of money . . ." Marisa said. She told everyone about the phone call she had received from Eric.

"Poor Eric," Bess said. "He's lucky he has Nancy on the case."

Marisa looked puzzled. "Why?"

"Nancy's a detective," Bess explained. "Didn't she tell you? She's been on tons of cases."

"Bess—" Nancy protested, embarrassed.

"Eric will be out of jail in no time," Bess promised. "You'll be going to the police station with Marisa, Nan—right?"

"I'd like to," Nancy said, "but I drove you and George here. How will you get home?"

"That's no problem," Devon said. He put his arm around Marisa. "I'll drive you and Marisa to the station, and—"

Marisa frowned. "That's okay, honey."

"No," Devon said. "I want to."

A clap of thunder was swiftly followed by a flash of lightning. Bess jumped.

"That was close," Nancy said.

Casey shivered against Bess's leg. "Poor baby," Bess said, scooping the puppy into her arms. "You're scared of thunder."

"We're going to be soaked if we don't make up our minds," George said. "If you'll let me drive your car, Nan, I'll take Bess, Amber, and Casey home."

"Fine with me," Nancy said. "And, actually, my father can take me home. He'll be meeting us at the police station. He wants to talk to Eric."

Marisa's grip on Misty's harness relaxed slightly. "I know Eric's innocent until proven guilty in the eyes of the law, but it means a lot to me that you and your dad are going to help clear

18

his name," she said to Nancy. "You hardly know me, and you've never even met Eric."

"I'm glad I can help," Nancy said. "Besides, there's nothing I love more than a good mystery."

Twenty minutes later Nancy flagged down her father when he stepped into the police station lobby. He walked over to them, his dripping umbrella leaving a trail of water across the floor. Nancy introduced him to Marisa and Devon.

"Pleased to meet you," Mr. Drew said. "I'm glad I was home when Nancy called. I came as soon as I could. I hope you haven't been waiting long."

"We just got here," Nancy said. "Do you think the police will let me see him today?"

"You have a good working relationship with Chief McGinnis," Mr. Drew said. "Let's see what he says."

Nancy had worked with Chief McGinnis on many cases in the past. She hoped he would be willing to bend the rules a little in this instance.

The chief passed through with a can of soda in his hand. "Hello, Drew family. What can we do for you today?"

Mr. Drew explained that he was Eric Pavlik's lawyer. "Any chance that Nancy could be present while I interview him?"

The chief nodded. "Why not? We brought him in for questioning, but he hasn't been for-

19

mally charged. We have a few more leads to pursue. However, the evidence against him is fairly strong."

Nancy introduced Marisa and Devon to Chief McGinnis.

"I don't suppose we could see Eric, too?" Marisa asked. "I'm a law student and a good friend—"

"Sure, go ahead," the chief agreed. "As I said, no charges have been filed at this time. We were planning to release him shortly. And if Mr. Pavlik isn't guilty, any help you can give us in breaking open this counterfeiting ring would be appreciated."

"Thanks, chief," Nancy said. "We'll do our best."

A few minutes later, a uniformed officer led Nancy, Mr. Drew, Marisa, and Devon into a large holding room. They sat down at the rectangular conference table. Misty laid her head across Marisa's feet and closed her eyes.

The officer brought Eric into the room. Eric had brown, curly hair and pale blue eyes, and appeared to Nancy to be in his early twenties. His corduroy blazer had a designer's emblem on the pocket.

Eric's eyes widened when he saw the group assembled in the room. "You can't all be here to see me," he said.

Mr. Drew stood up and went over to Eric. "I'm

Carson Drew," he said, and reached for Eric's hand.

Eric shook it. "Pleased to meet you. Thank you so much for your help, Mr. Drew."

Mr. Drew smiled. "I haven't done anything yet." He turned to Nancy. "This is my daughter, Nancy. She's an amateur detective, and Marisa has asked her to help with your case. And I'm here in case you need a lawyer."

Eric sat down at the table. "Great. I have the feeling I can use all the help I can get."

"You don't mind *our* being here, do you?" Marisa asked.

Eric shook his head. "Of course not."

"Even me?" Devon asked.

Nancy looked at Devon. She thought she heard the hint of a challenge in his voice.

"We're fraternity brothers," Eric said. "I don't have anything to hide from you."

"Okay, Eric," Mr. Drew said. "Why don't we start from the beginning?"

"Yes, Mr. Drew." Eric took a deep breath. "I was at the mall, buying a present for Marisa's birthday, which is on Friday."

"At which store?" Mr. Drew asked.

"Close your ears, Marisa," Eric said.

Marisa obligingly plugged her ears with her fingers.

"Ledbetter's Jewelers," Eric whispered. "I was buying a silver bracelet." He reached over

21

and gently pulled Marisa's hands from her ears. Nancy saw a dark look cross Devon's face.

"Okay," Eric told Marisa. "You can listen now. I paid for the gift, but the clerk kept stalling. Finally, two mall security officers came and told me they thought two of the twenty-dollar bills I had given them were counterfeit. They took me to the security office, and then the police came and brought me to the station."

"Any idea where you got the counterfeit bills?" Mr. Drew asked.

Eric shrugged. "I went to the bank on campus yesterday morning. I also got change at the Westmoor bookstore when I bought some school supplies."

"You're a student at Westmoor University?" Mr. Drew asked.

"Yes, sir," Eric replied.

"And your major?"

"I'm a junior majoring in architecture," Eric said. "My minor is business."

"Do you get good grades?"

"Mostly A's," Eric replied.

"Do you have a part-time job?"

Eric shook his head. "Nothing steady. I do a few odd jobs here and there. And I volunteer."

"Anything else you'd like to add?" Mr. Drew asked.

Eric shook his head. "No, sir. That's all I know."

Mr. Drew handed Eric his business card. "If you think of anything else, call me. Otherwise, I'll be in touch with you tomorrow."

Eric stood up. "Thank you for your help."

"The chief said you'd be released shortly," Mr. Drew said. "Please don't answer any questions about the case unless I'm with you."

"Yes, sir," Eric said. "I mean—no, sir. Thank you, Mr. Drew." Eric stood up and pumped Mr. Drew's hand.

Back in the lobby, Nancy said goodbye to Marisa and Devon. Marisa gave Nancy her phone number. "Please call me if you get any new information."

"I will," Nancy promised.

Nancy rode home with her father. The rain had slowed to a drizzle, and the windshield wipers made a comforting, swishing sound.

"I've been following this counterfeiting business pretty closely in the newspapers," Mr. Drew said. "How about you?"

Nancy shook her head. "Not really. I've read one or two articles."

"Well," Mr. Drew said, "there's been quite a bit of counterfeit money in circulation in River Heights recently. Most of it has turned up at the mall, the Westmoor campus bookstore, Café Olé . . ."

"The Mexican restaurant on University Boulevard?" Nancy asked.

Mr. Drew nodded.

"So a Westmoor student must be the most likely suspect," Nancy said.

"Yes. A couple of Westmoor students have been picked up for questioning after passing phony bills, but they were released."

"Chief McGinnis said the evidence against Eric was fairly strong," Nancy said. "What do you think he meant?"

"Besides being caught in the act of passing the phony bills, Eric's an architecture student—an A student," Mr. Drew said. "I would imagine he has the drafting skills one would need to pull off a convincing forgery."

"Drafting skills?" Nancy turned to her father. "Dad, don't most counterfeiters use laser printers or photocopiers? I didn't think they drafted the bills themselves."

"That's generally true," Mr. Drew said. "But I've read that the police feel this is an old-fashioned and well-executed job. I presume that means the bills were drafted by hand."

"You asked Eric if he has a job," Nancy said. "I guess you're wondering where he got the money to buy an expensive birthday present for Marisa. And did you see those designer clothes he was wearing?"

Mr. Drew chuckled. "Were they designer clothes? My sense of young people's fashions is

24

not too keen. But you're right. Most college students are strapped for cash."

"Maybe he has rich parents," Nancy said.

"Maybe."

When they pulled into the driveway, Nancy saw that George had returned the Mustang. "I think I'll go to the library," she said.

"Didn't you just go yesterday?" her father asked.

"Yesterday was for pleasure reading. Today is for information," Nancy said.

"And you'll be a counterfeiting expert by morning," Mr. Drew said.

Nancy grinned. "I hope so."

George had left Nancy's car keys with the Drews' housekeeper, Hannah Gruen. Nancy retrieved them and drove to the central library.

Nancy searched the computer catalogue and found one book on crime that contained a chapter on counterfeiting. She sighed. This was not a promising start. She had to read some back issues of the River Heights *Morning Record* to learn more about this counterfeiting case.

In the reference section, Nancy picked through her change purse for quarters and dropped them into a microfiche reader. The newspaper index listed seven recent articles on counterfeiting. There were also four articles dating from twenty-five years earlier.

After reading the first seven pieces, Nancy searched for the four older articles. Unfortunately, the library had only the last two in the group. Nancy pulled up the older one first. She read the headline with interest: "Westmoor University Center of Police Investigation in Counterfeiting Case."

The article described a number of counterfeiting incidents in River Heights and surrounding cities. Many of the counterfeit bills had turned up at Westmoor University. Because of the high quality of the forgery, the police were looking for an expert draftsman. The article also said that a Westmoor student had been held for questioning but was released due to lack of evidence. Because he was a minor, the newspaper did not print his name.

"Arrests Made in Counterfeiting Case" read the headline of the second article. Two months after the Westmoor student was questioned, a state trooper had pulled over a milk truck with a faulty taillight. The trooper found $100,000 worth of counterfeit twenty-dollar bills in the back of the truck. The driver, Frank Goetz, and an accomplice, Don Blevins, were arrested.

The two men confessed that they were transporting the phony money to Chicago, as they had done several times before. However, both men claimed no responsibility for printing the counterfeit money. Goetz worked as a cook and Blevins as a gardener, and the police believed neither had the skills to accomplish such expert forgery. But the suspects refused to name their boss, the forger and mastermind of the counterfeiting ring. Police had agreed to reduce the charges against them in exchange for information, but so far Blevins and Goetz weren't talking.

Nancy turned off the microfiche reader. If this was the last article, she thought, Blevins and Goetz had probably never revealed the name of their boss. Twenty-five years had passed. What had happened? Did the counterfeiter stop printing the phony money? And more important, could there be a connection between the old case and the recent one?

Nancy pondered this question while she checked out her library book and drove home. The details of the two counterfeiting cases seemed similar. But what about the Westmoor University connection? Obviously, if the counterfeiter of twenty-five years ago had been a student, he or she would no longer be a student today. Why was so much of the present-day phony money circulating around Westmoor? Could a staff member be the guilty party? Or maybe there was no connection between the two counterfeiting cases at all.

At home, Nancy found her father working in his study. She told him what she had learned at the library.

"So the mastermind of the old counterfeiting ring was never caught," Mr. Drew said.

"I don't think so. I'd like to check with the police," Nancy said.

"Maybe we should check something else with the police." Mr. Drew stood and pulled his wallet from his back pocket. He took out a wrinkled twenty-dollar bill. " 'Series 1993,' " he read. "Does that mean it was printed in 1993?"

Nancy skimmed through the chapter in the library book about counterfeiting. "Not necessarily. It means that 1993 was the year the design for that bill was approved. So it was printed sometime between then and now. It says here that the series date usually changes every few years."

"Hmm . . ." Mr. Drew said. "I wonder . . ."

Nancy finished his thought. "I wonder what date is printed on the bills Eric had when he was arrested?"

Mr. Drew reached for the phone. "I'll call Detective Lee, the officer in charge of the investigation."

Two minutes later he had an answer. "Nancy, your theory is right on the money. Both of Eric's counterfeit bills are dated twenty-five years ago."

3

Money, Money Everywhere

"Eric wasn't even born twenty-five years ago. That should let him off the hook, right?" Nancy said.

"Absolutely." Mr. Drew put back the file folder he had been flipping through. "And that means there most likely is a connection between the two counterfeiting cases."

"What did the police say about the first counterfeiting case?"

"They didn't know anything about it. Their computer files don't go back that far, and none of the vice officers has been on the squad for twenty-five years. Detective Lee said they're going to try to dig up the old files in storage."

"Did he say how long it would take?"

"Why do you ask that?" Mr. Drew turned and looked Nancy in the eye. "Wait a minute. You've just cleared Eric's name. That was your job. Aren't you off the case now?"

Nancy sighed. "I can't leave a mystery half-solved. Besides, there will always be questions about Eric's innocence until the real counterfeiter's caught."

"Not in the eyes of the law," Mr. Drew said.

"No, but he did pass those phony bills, after all. I wonder whether they came from the batch of money printed twenty-five years ago. After all, someone could have made new bills with the old engraved plates."

"I'll ask Detective Lee tomorrow if forensics can determine how old the bills are. In the meantime, I'm going to call Eric and give him the good news."

"And then I'll call Marisa," Nancy said.

Marisa sounded breathless when she answered the phone. "Hello?"

"Marisa, this is Nancy Drew. I hope this isn't a bad time."

"No. I was just talking to Devon on the other line. Any news?"

Nancy filled Marisa in on what had happened.

"Bess said you were a good detective, but I had no idea. . . ."

"The case isn't solved yet," Nancy said. "And I'd like to keep working on it a little longer."

"That's great!" Marisa exclaimed. "I really want to clear Eric's name completely. I'll do whatever I can to help you."

"Thanks," Nancy said. "Could you answer one question for me? Are Eric's parents rich?"

"Not especially," Marisa said. "But if you're wondering about his financial resources, Eric's terrific with money."

"I remember he said he's minoring in business. That makes sense."

They chatted for a few more minutes. "I'd better go study," Marisa finally said. "Thanks for calling, Nancy."

"I'll talk to you soon," Nancy said. She hung up the phone.

That night, Nancy read the counterfeiting chapter from her library book before going to sleep. She spent the night dreaming about money—piles and piles of money.

Nancy was awakened at seven the next morning by the ringing telephone. "Hello?" she mumbled.

"Nan? Did I wake you?"

"Hi, Bess." Nancy propped her pillow behind her and sat up. "It's okay. What are you doing up at this hour?"

Bess sighed. "Casey woke me up at two. And at four. And at six. I finally gave up on sleep."

"How's the housebreaking going?"

Bess cleared her throat. "Don't ask. Would you like to come over?"

"May I take my shower first?" Nancy asked.

"Oh—sure. Sorry. And, Nan?"

Nancy smiled. "Yes?"

"You might want to wear a different pair of shoes today. I read a few more chapters of my dog-training book. Apparently, dogs like to repeat accidents in the same spot."

"Thanks for telling me," Nancy said with a chuckle. "I'll see you in a little while."

After breakfast Hannah packed up a basket of blueberry muffins for Nancy to take to Bess.

"Thanks, Hannah." Nancy rinsed her cereal bowl and put it in the dishwasher. "Bess loves your muffins as much as I do."

Hannah handed Nancy another small bundle tied with a red ribbon. "These are dog biscuits for Casey. I couldn't find a recipe, so I'm afraid they're store-bought."

Nancy laughed. "That was very thoughtful of you. Something tells me Casey's going to be a spoiled puppy."

When Nancy arrived at Bess's house, the Marvins were eating breakfast. Casey sat on Bess's lap.

"She doesn't have her own chair?" Nancy asked.

"Very funny," Bess said. "She kept whining, so I finally had to pick her up."

Nancy set Hannah's muffins on the table, out of Casey's reach. Bess peeked into the basket. "Hannah's muffins. Yum." She pulled Casey away from the table. "You have your own treats," she said as she gave Casey a dog biscuit.

"Please thank Hannah for us, Nancy," Mrs. Marvin said. "This was very sweet of her."

"I will," Nancy said.

Mr. Marvin sneezed.

"Bless you," Nancy and Bess said. Mrs. Marvin passed him the pitcher of orange juice.

Bess poured her father a glass of juice while he got up to blow his nose. "Dad's getting a cold—just in time for his vacation," Bess said.

"I'm hoping to nip it in the bud with lots of fresh Florida oranges." Mr. Marvin returned to the table and downed the juice.

"You're going to Florida?" Nancy asked.

Mrs. Marvin nodded. "We're visiting friends in Miami. We're leaving this afternoon."

"Before I forget to ask you," Bess said to her mother, "Marisa wanted to know if I'd like to have her grandmother's antique sewing machine. What do you think?"

"Is she sure she wants to part with it?" Mrs. Marvin asked.

Bess nodded. "She offered to give it to me, but I'd like to pay her for it. It's beautiful."

"That sounds like a wonderful idea," Mrs. Marvin said.

The doorbell rang. "I'll get it," Mr. Marvin said. He stopped in the kitchen to snatch a tissue on the way to the door.

A moment later Amber bounded into the dining room. "Hi, Casey."

"Say, 'Hi, Amber,'" Bess told the puppy. She

33

set Casey on the ground, and the puppy jumped up on Amber's legs.

A man in his forties followed Mr. Marvin into the dining room. "This must be Casey."

Amber nodded. "Isn't she beautiful, Daddy?"

"She is cute. Look at the size of those feet. That means she's going to be a big girl."

Bess introduced Nancy to Amber and Devon's father, Larry Marshall. Mr. Marshall shook Nancy's hand. "Pleased to meet you."

"May we take Casey for a walk?" Amber asked Bess.

"I would be thrilled if you would take Casey for a walk," Bess said. She went into the kitchen to get the leash.

After the Marshalls had left with Casey, Mr. and Mrs. Marvin went into their bedroom to finish packing. "I'm going to call Marisa," Bess told Nancy. "Maybe I can pick up the sewing machine today."

A few minutes later, it had been arranged that Nancy and Bess would meet Marisa at Candlelight Inn to get the sewing machine while Amber dog-sat Casey at the Marshalls' house.

Bess set out a handful of treats and gathered Casey's toys. "Do you think you'll need anything else?" she asked Amber.

"No. But if we do, my dad has a key to your house," Amber said. "Casey and I will be fine. Right, Casey?"

Casey licked Amber's face.

Mr. Marshall frowned. "Amber, is that sanitary? Don't let your mother see that."

Amber laughed. "Don't worry. I know I'd never be allowed to get a puppy if she saw Casey doing that."

At the inn, Bess and Nancy found Marisa, Misty, and Penny Rosen in the study. Marisa's fingertips flew across a document in Braille. "There's no mention of a service contract for the furnace," she was saying.

Penny flipped through a stack of papers in her lap. "It says here the furnace was manufactured in 1952. Even if there was a service contract, I imagine it has expired by now."

Bess cleared her throat to announce their arrival. "Hi. The door was unlocked, so we let ourselves in."

Marisa turned around. "Hi, Bess. Did you bring Casey?"

"No. Mercifully, Amber is watching her," Bess said.

Penny smiled. "Puppies are a handful, aren't they?"

"And then some." Bess walked over to pet Misty. "You're so nice and calm, Misty. Is Casey ever going to be like you?"

"We hope so," Penny said.

"How's it going?" Nancy asked.

"Not so well," Marisa said. "We knew the inn would need a lot of renovation, but . . ."

"The building's very old," Penny explained. "And Marisa's grandmother never made many of the upgrades we need in a facility that will house people with visual impairments. For example, we'll need to install an electromagnetic stove in the kitchen that can heat food without a heating element. The bathrooms will need rails—"

"And probably new plumbing," Marisa said. "The furnace isn't heating the whole house efficiently. There's no central air conditioning, and there isn't adequate lighting for the sighted guests."

Penny set down her pencil. "I hate to say this, Marisa, but I'm beginning to wonder if this is a mistake."

"What do you mean?" Marisa asked, concern in her voice.

"These renovations are going to cost much more than we've budgeted. Frankly, I don't know whether the Guiding Eyes can afford it. And I wonder whether your grandmother's money might be better spent on upkeep of other facilities the Guiding Eyes is already operating."

"I'm not a lawyer yet," Marisa said, "so I might be wrong. But it's my understanding that since Grandmother specifically requested that her money be used to open a school in River Heights, and since you agreed to that condition before she died, you and the Guiding Eyes have to do your best to follow her wishes."

"We *will* do our best," Penny said. "Believe me. It's just—"

A short woman wearing a hard hat, work boots, and jeans entered the room. "Oh, I'm sorry. I didn't realize you had visitors," she said.

Penny introduced Nancy and Bess to Joan Bland. "Joan's a contractor," she explained. "She's estimating the cost of the renovations."

"I'm a little perplexed," Joan said. "I've triple-checked my measurements, and it appears there's a hidden space in one of the second-floor bedrooms. It must have been walled-over during an earlier remodeling."

Penny, Marisa, Misty, Nancy, and Bess followed Joan upstairs to the bedroom. "It's right back here." Joan tapped the wall, which sounded hollow.

Marisa moved toward the wall and nearly tripped on a loose floorboard. Misty hung her head. "It's okay, Misty. It's not your fault I tripped. I guess Devon never finished fixing this," she said.

Nancy spotted a walk-in closet on the adjoining wall. "Do you have a flashlight?" she asked Joan.

Joan found a flashlight and a hammer in her toolbox. As Nancy shone the flashlight around the inside of the closet, Joan went to work patching the loose floorboard.

Bess poked her head inside the dark closet. She wrinkled her nose at the stale smell as she pushed aside clothes that had obviously not been worn in many years. A cloud of dust rose in the air.

Bess shrieked. "What was that?"

Nancy jumped. "What?"

"Something just ran up my arm!"

"It was probably just a spider," Nancy said.

"S-spider?" Bess stammered. She hastily backed out of the closet, brushing frantically at her clothing.

"Did you find anything?" Marisa asked.

Nancy tugged on a square wall panel. "Yes. I think this is some sort of hidden entrance, but I can't get it open."

Nancy knew that a lot of old houses had secret rooms and hidden passageways. She had an idea. "Joan?" she called. "Do you think you could tug on that floorboard out there?"

Joan pulled the floorboard upward. After a few inches, it made a sound like a gunshot, and the panel in the closet creaked open.

"It's okay, Misty," Marisa murmured.

Nancy tugged the panel away from the wall and brushed away several cobwebs. She shone the flashlight through the large opening and gasped at what she saw.

Stacked neatly from floor to ceiling in the tiny room were piles and piles of money.

4

Inn Debt

With a shaking hand, Nancy pulled out a packet of money. She sneezed as the dust tickled her nose. One by one, she examined the twenty-dollar bills in her hand. Every one of them was twenty-five years old.

Nancy clutched the money to her chest and backed out of the closet. "Look what I found."

"What is it?" Marisa asked. Still frightened by the noisy floorboard, Misty shook at her side.

"Oh—I'm sorry," Nancy said, realizing that Marisa could not see what she held in her hand. She explained about the money. "And there must be thousands of dollars still in the closet."

"What are we going to do?" Bess asked.

"We're going to call the police. I'll bet anything that this money's counterfeit." Nancy held one of the bills underneath a lamp. "Aside from the fact that it happens to be twenty-five years old," Nancy said, "it doesn't have the red and blue fibers embedded in the paper that genuine currency should have."

Detective Lee arrived at the inn within half an hour. He examined several of the bills under a magnifying glass. "This is an excellent forgery. But all of these bills have the same serial number," he said. "No two bills in the same series should have matching serial numbers. No doubt about it, this money is counterfeit. And," he added, "these bills have the same serial number as the two we found on Eric Pavlik. Judging from all this dust, they were probably printed around the same time."

"Eric's counterfeit money was printed twenty-five years ago?" Nancy asked.

"Yes. Forensics confirmed it this morning."

"Too bad it's counterfeit money. I guess a secret stash of thousands of *real* dollars was too much to hope for." Penny sighed. "That money really would have helped us with repairs to the inn. It has a lot of structural problems," she explained to Detective Lee.

"It has a lot of problems, period," the detective said. He gestured toward the closet. "Based on what I see here, I would bet that Candlelight Inn was the center of operations for the old counterfeiting ring."

40

Nancy thought that Detective Lee was probably right. "But who was the counterfeiter?" she asked. "And how did Eric wind up with the money?"

"No offense, Ms. Henares," Detective Lee said, "but your grandmother would be the obvious suspect—except that she passed away shortly before the counterfeit bills reappeared in River Heights."

"She had no ties to Westmoor University," Penny said.

"Except for Marisa," Detective Lee said. "Besides your grandmother, who had access to the inn?" he asked Marisa.

"I—I don't know. I moved to River Heights last year from Milwaukee to go to law school." Marisa took a deep breath. "My mother and my grandmother were estranged before I was born. My parents died two years ago, and that's when I met my grandmother for the first time. She was a very private person, Detective. Even though I saw her many times before she died, I didn't know much about her personal life. She did have a housekeeper, but I never met her. I'm afraid I don't remember her name."

"I understand it came as a great shock to many people that Mrs. Whitby was a multimillionaire," Detective Lee said.

"Yes," Marisa said. "She paid for my law school education, but even I had no idea how wealthy she was. Apparently, she earned the money by investing in stocks over many years."

Detective Lee scribbled in his pocket notepad. "Okay. Thanks for your help, Ms. Henares, Ms. Drew. I'll be in touch."

Penny showed Detective Lee to the door.

"You haven't found any useful information in your grandmother's personal papers?" Nancy asked Marisa.

"No," Marisa said. "Of course, I've only gone through about a quarter of them so far. Even with Penny's help, it's quite a job."

"Would you like me to help?" Nancy offered.

"That's very kind of you," Marisa said. "Unfortunately, unless you read Braille, you won't be able to get far."

"I don't read Braille," Nancy said. "But please let me know if there's anything else I can do."

Marisa smiled. "Didn't you and Bess come to get a sewing machine? You've wasted half your day here already. I feel terrible."

"It's not your fault," Nancy said. "I only hope it fits in my car."

With the convertible top down, the sewing machine fit into the backseat. Finding a place to put it in Bess's room half an hour later was more difficult.

Casey and Amber supervised as Nancy and Bess moved the desk underneath the window and the sewing machine into the corner where the desk had been.

Nancy patted the sewing machine. "You'd better get a lot of use out of this."

Amber giggled as Casey licked her bare toes. "That tickles."

"Thanks for watching Casey for so long, Amber," Bess said. "Nancy brought us some delicious muffins this morning. Do you want to take some home?"

Amber's face fell. "Do I have to go?"

Bess reached over and squeaked Casey's hamburger. "Not if you don't want to."

Amber sighed. "I guess it's time anyway. Maybe Devon and Marisa will take me to the mall with them."

The trio headed for the kitchen, where Bess put some muffins in a bag and handed them to Amber. "'Bye, Amber. Thanks again. Come visit soon."

"'Bye, Bess. 'Bye, Nancy," Amber called.

Nancy and Bess watched through the window while Amber walked to her house. "Poor Amber," Bess said. "I don't think she's too happy at home."

"That's a shame."

Bess nodded. "I know. The Marshalls have been having a lot of financial troubles lately. Mr. Marshall's a land developer and a builder, and his business has been doing poorly. I think Devon moved back home from his fraternity house to cut down on his college costs. And Mr. Marshall doesn't approve of his relationship with Marisa, so it's been rough on everyone."

"How could anyone not like Marisa?" Nancy asked.

Bess shrugged. "That's a good question. She's one of the nicest people I've ever met."

An hour later Nancy breathed in the comforting aroma of Hannah's homemade chicken noodle soup. Nancy's mother had died when she was very young, and she was grateful for the love and support she had from her father and from Hannah.

"Hannah, your soup smells wonderful," Nancy said.

Hannah smiled. "One of the Homemakers gave me a new recipe."

Hannah had many good friends in the River Heights Homemakers club, and like Hannah, all of them were excellent cooks.

Nancy had an idea. "Hannah—do you know if any of the Homemakers ever worked as a housekeeper for Emmaline Whitby?"

Hannah set down her dish towel. "The woman who owned Candlelight Inn? Yes, as a matter of fact, Kay McNamara worked for Mrs. Whitby for years."

"Do you have her phone number?" Nancy asked.

Hannah rolled her eyes. "What are you getting yourself into now, Nancy?"

Nancy smiled. She knew Hannah worried about her. "Nothing dangerous, I promise. I'm just trying to learn who had access to Candlelight Inn. And your friend, Mrs. McNamara, might be able to tell me."

Mrs. McNamara was home when Nancy called her. She said she would be happy to speak with Nancy the next morning.

Nancy phoned Marisa, who asked if she could accompany Nancy to see Mrs. McNamara.

"Sure," Nancy said. She took down the directions to Marisa's apartment and arranged to pick her up at eight-thirty the next morning.

Mrs. McNamara was a stout woman, in her sixties or seventies, Nancy figured.

"I hope this isn't an inconvenience for you," Nancy said after introductions were made.

"None whatsoever," Mrs. McNamara said. She ushered them into her spotless living room. "I'm so pleased to meet you, Marisa. I was very fond of your grandmother, you know. It's odd we never met before."

"It *is* odd," Marisa agreed. "But my grandmother didn't like to share too much of her personal life." She sat down with Misty at her feet.

45

Mrs. McNamara nodded. "That's certainly true. I worked for her for over forty years, and I know very little. I'm afraid I won't be able to answer many of your questions."

"Do you know if anyone else worked for Mrs. Whitby?" Nancy asked.

"I don't think so," Mrs. McNamara said. "Of course, I can't be sure. I came in once a week to do the heavy cleaning. Mrs. Whitby did everything else herself." She chuckled. "Of course, she did eat a lot of prepared food. Even before she lost her sight, she wasn't much of a cook."

Marisa shifted in her chair. "Most legally blind people need at least a little help with their bookkeeping. I know I do. My grandmother didn't have anyone?"

"She may have had someone to help manage her finances," Mrs. McNamara said. "But it wasn't me, and I haven't the faintest idea who it might have been. Now, years ago, when she still had some sight, I think Susan—your mother—was involved with the bookkeeping. She was a sweet girl, but then . . ." Mrs. McNamara shook her head. "I know your grandmother's deepest regret was losing touch with her only child. Mrs. Whitby didn't talk about what happened, but she was never the same afterward. I'm so glad you were able to get to know your grandmother, Marisa. How is your mother, dear?"

Marisa closed her eyes. "She died two years ago."

Mrs. McNamara reached out and touched Marisa's arm. "I'm so sorry."

Marisa choked back a sob. Nancy hastily stood up. "Thank you for your help, Mrs. McNamara. We'd better be going."

Nancy led Marisa and Misty to the car. "Are you okay?" Nancy asked as they buckled their seat belts.

Marisa wiped the tears from her cheeks. "Yes. It makes me so sad that my mother and grandmother never resolved their differences. I'm sorry I got so emotional in there. You probably wanted to ask Mrs. McNamara more questions."

"No," Nancy said. "I could tell she really didn't have much information."

"If you don't have any plans this morning, will you let me cook you breakfast?" Marisa asked.

Nancy smiled. "I'd love it. Thanks."

A little while later, Nancy found a space on University Boulevard and parallel parked her car across from Marisa's apartment building. She looked both ways for traffic while Misty and Marisa stood on the curb.

"It's clear," Nancy said. She stepped off the curb.

"No—" Marisa said.

Misty whined and nudged Nancy backward.

A black sports car sped around the corner, tires screeching. It streaked down the street and careened onto a side road, out of sight.

Nancy gasped. Her heart was pounding. If Misty hadn't kept her from crossing the street, the car would have hit her. Where was that person going in such a hurry? Nancy hadn't had time to see the license plate or even the make of the car.

"Thank you, Misty," she said.

Marisa bent and hugged her dog. "Good girl, Misty. Good girl. Misty would never let us cross the street until it was really okay," she said to Nancy.

Misty stepped off the curb.

"Okay, Misty. You're the boss," Nancy said. She and Marisa followed Misty across the street.

By the time they reached Marisa's apartment, Nancy's heartbeat had returned to its normal rate. Marisa and Misty led her on a tour of their small apartment.

"Everything is so well organized," Nancy said.

"It has to be," Marisa explained. "Not that I usually show people my closet, but . . ." She threw open her closet door.

Nancy reached out and fingered a silky purple dress. "This purple dress is gorgeous."

Marisa smiled. "Thanks. Devon bought it for me. I love the way it feels. It's also so distinctive, it helps me find my way around my closet. You will note that neatness is the key to getting by when you can't see."

Nancy noticed that Marisa's wardrobe was arranged completely by color. Different colors hung on different types of hangers.

"My kitchen is the same way," Marisa explained. "And if someone ever puts something back in the wrong place, I'm completely thrown. My grandmother gave Misty a can of dog biscuits shortly before she died, and Devon set them next to my cookie jar. Have you ever taken a bite of a dog biscuit?"

Nancy laughed. "Yuck."

"Tell me about it," Marisa said.

Nancy noticed the computer on Marisa's desk. It had speakers, a CD-ROM drive, and an external modem. "This is pretty spiffy," she said.

"I type, and it reads the words back to me," Marisa said. "It's incredible." She turned it on and tapped out some letters on the keypad. As the words appeared on the screen, a male voice said, "Hello, Nancy."

"That's amazing," Nancy said.

"I'd never get through law school without it." Marisa led Nancy back to the living room. Braille textbooks and audiobooks were stacked on the coffee table.

"It's a little cluttered," Marisa said. "Sorry. I was studying this morning. I like to catch up on my work while I'm doing my chores."

She pushed the Play button on her tape recorder as she entered the kitchen. "This is my Criminal Procedures tape. Listen to what it says about counterfeiting."

After a moment of silence, a voice came from the tape player. It was the flat, male voice of Marisa's talking computer: "I'm watching you, Marisa. Stop playing detective, or your days will be numbered."

5

Recipe for Disaster

With a shaking hand, Marisa pressed the Stop button.

"Wait," Nancy said. "You'd better not touch that. The police will want to dust for fingerprints."

"Who's calling the police?" Marisa stabbed the Eject button with her finger and yanked out the tape.

"Marisa," Nancy said gently, "someone has just made a threat on your life."

"Obviously this person doesn't want me— us—working on the counterfeiting case. That only makes me want to work harder." Marisa turned to face Nancy. "What about you?"

"Well—" Nancy began.

"Do you want the police to tell us to leave the case to professionals?"

"No, but—"

"I know you wouldn't give up, and neither will I," Marisa said. "Now, tell me—do you see any signs of forced entry?"

Nancy examined the lock on the front door carefully. "No. And your building has security code entry. It would have been difficult to break in. Does anyone else have a key or know the code?" she asked.

Marisa sat down on the sofa. "Just Devon," she said. "And my landlord, of course."

"Is it possible your landlord may have let someone into your apartment?" Nancy asked.

"I doubt it." Marisa pulled the phone toward her. "But we have been expecting a plumber to work on the pipes. I'll call my landlord and check."

She pressed an automatic dial button on her phone, which had large numbers labeled in Braille.

Briefly, Marisa explained to her landlord what had happened. She shook her head as she hung up the phone. "No. I knew he wouldn't let anyone in without my permission."

Nancy sighed. "Okay. Next, I want to check your computer."

Marisa explained to Nancy how the system worked. In the main word-processing directory,

Nancy found a file that had been saved that morning. According to the time code, it was a few minutes before Nancy and Marisa had returned to the apartment.

Nancy retrieved the file. As she moved the cursor across the screen, the computer voice read the same chilling message: "I'm watching you, Marisa. Stop playing detective, or your days will be numbered."

Marisa reached out and turned off the computer without even bothering to exit the program. "I don't think I'd like to hear that again."

"I agree with you," Nancy said. "But we just learned something very interesting. We can now assume that someone got into your apartment, typed the threatening message, taped the voice of the computer reading the words, then substituted the tape for your audiobook. What we don't know is why someone would go to so much trouble to scare you. Or who it might be. Come to think of it," she added, "whoever zoomed by us in the sports car just before we came up to your apartment is a good suspect. Anyone making a getaway would be in a hurry, and the intruder must have left just before we got back."

Marisa bit her lip. "Whoever broke in, it's obviously someone who doesn't know me well. Otherwise, he or she would realize that I don't scare easily."

"You have a point," Nancy said. "Marisa—I

know you're determined to keep working on the case, but I hope you're not planning to stay here by yourself."

"Of course I am," Marisa said.

"I don't mean to frighten you," Nancy said, "but if someone has access to your building, and says he or she is watching you, it doesn't seem safe . . ."

"I can take care of myself," Marisa said firmly. "And Misty's a great watchdog."

"All right," Nancy said. "Will you at least promise to call me tonight and check in?"

Marisa stood up and headed for the kitchen. "Even better—would you like to come to dinner with me and Bess and Casey? We're going to Café Olé. Devon's a waiter there, and he's scheduled to work tonight."

"I don't have any plans," Nancy said, following her. Her boyfriend, Ned Nickerson, was busy studying for his midterm exams at Emerson College. Nancy was looking forward to spending time with him after he finished his exams.

In the kitchen, Nancy poured two glasses of cranberry juice as Marisa used a cutting guide and a knife to slice fresh strawberries.

"Wait a minute," Nancy said. "Did you just say Casey's coming tonight?"

Marisa rinsed her hands. "Bess is supposed to get her used to behaving in public places, like restaurants. After all, if Casey passes her guide dog training, she'll be spending a lot of time in malls, restaurants—you name it."

"Is she housebroken yet?" Nancy asked.

"I hope so." Marisa laughed. "If not, we may not be welcome at Café Olé ever again."

Casey sniffed a small patch of grass outside Café Olé that evening as Bess, Nancy, and George watched anxiously. Casey wore a bright yellow vest that identified her as a guide-dog-in-training.

"I'm glad you were able to join us for dinner, George," Marisa said.

"Me, too. If we ever get to eat dinner." George looked at Bess. "Bess, she's not going to go. She just went to the bathroom five minutes ago."

"She hasn't had an accident all day, and we're not about to start in the restaurant. You wouldn't go either if all these people were staring at you," Bess said. "You just take your time, Casey."

Casey took her time, but she did finally satisfy Bess by squatting in the grass for two seconds. The group then entered the restaurant.

A hostess wearing a frilly, flowered dress greeted them. "Hi, Marisa," she said. "There's only one table left in Devon's station, and I saved it for you."

"Thanks, Ally." Marisa smiled. "Devon's a popular waiter," she told Nancy, Bess, and George. "His tables always fill up quickly."

55

"Wow," Bess said as they were led through the crowded restaurant. "This place is busy."

Nancy breathed in the rich aroma of spices and coffee. "And it smells great."

George laughed. "Casey and Misty think so, too."

Both dogs' noses twitched, and their tails were in the air. "I can tell when Misty's paying a little too much attention to her surroundings," Marisa said. "She walks more slowly."

Misty settled across Marisa's feet when they were seated at a table near the kitchen. A busboy brought everyone menus and filled their glasses with water. Casey playfully nipped at his feet.

"Casey, be a good girl," Bess said as she tugged on the dog's leash. Casey's tail wagged, and she darted under the table.

Misty yelped. "Casey!" Bess said sharply. She poked her head under the table.

"It's okay, Bess." Marisa patted Misty's head. "She didn't do anything. Misty's been edgy all day."

"Because of the break-in?" Nancy asked.

"Break-in?" Bess's head popped up. "What break-in?"

Nancy explained what had happened at Marisa's apartment that morning.

Bess shook her head. "And of course you two are going to keep working on the case. Why do a sensible thing like worry about your safety?"

"If the counterfeiter's trying to scare you off the case, you must be close to the truth," George said. "Do you have any new leads?"

"Not really," Nancy said. "We're just trying to figure out who had access to the inn and could have stashed the counterfeit money there."

"Do you think it may have been a guest?" George asked.

"The inn was already closed twenty-five years ago when the counterfeit bills were printed," Marisa said.

Bess pried her dinner napkin from Casey's mouth. "Maybe a former guest kept a key."

"At this point, it could have been anyone," Nancy said.

Misty began to sniff the air furiously. She stood up and wagged her tail.

"Here comes Devon," Marisa said.

A moment later Devon walked past with a heavy tray. He squeezed Marisa's arm as he passed, and she smiled. "I'll be right back," he said. "Study those menus."

"I'm sorry, Marisa," Bess said. "Do you need me to read you the menu?"

"No, thanks," Marisa said. "I come here often enough, I practically have it memorized. I always get the same thing, anyhow."

"That would be the tortilla soup, chicken quesadillas, and flan for dessert." Eric Pavlik had entered the restaurant with a group of friends.

They had moved to a table and sat down, but Eric stopped behind Marisa's chair. "Am I right?"

"You're right." Marisa smiled. "What are you doing here? Shouldn't you be studying for your calc midterm?"

"Of course I should," Eric said. "But I couldn't concentrate, so I decided to go out tonight with friends—get my mind off things. Anyhow, we have lots of last-minute plans to make for the 5K run that our fraternity's sponsoring tomorrow morning."

"You're Beta Tau? I'm running in your 5K," George said.

"And we all pledged money," Bess added. "I didn't know your fraternity was the sponsor. How come Devon didn't mention it?" she asked Marisa.

"I don't know," Marisa said.

"He's been so busy, I'm not sure he even remembers. But it's a pretty big event. We hope to raise at least five thousand dollars for the Guiding Eyes school," Eric said. "By the way, I heard about the counterfeit money you found at the inn. Have you had any more leads, Marisa?"

"Not yet, but—" Marisa stopped as Misty's tail beat against her legs. "What is it, Misty?"

Just then Amber and her parents entered the restaurant. "Look who's here!" Amber cried. She ran to the table and dropped to her knees to pet Casey and Misty.

"Amber," Mrs. Marshall said, "is this how we behave in a restaurant?"

"Sorry, Mom." Amber got to her feet and brushed off her knees. "We're here to visit Devon," she told Marisa. "You, too?"

"Yes," Marisa said. "He's busy tonight. We haven't even ordered yet, and I need to go to the ladies' room. Would you mind ordering for me if Devon comes back while I'm gone?"

"No problem," Bess said.

Eric watched Marisa and Misty until they were out of earshot. "Perfect," he said. "I'm glad I got the chance to tell you this all at once. Some college friends and I are throwing a surprise birthday party here for Marisa on Friday night. It's at eight o'clock. I hope you can make it."

"I'm afraid we have plans that night, Eric," Mr. Marshall said, "but thank you for thinking of us."

"What plans?" Amber asked. "I want to go to Marisa's party."

"Come on, Amber," her mother said. "Let's go find our table, and we'll talk about it."

The Marshalls and Eric left for their respective tables as Devon approached with his order pad.

"Welcome to Café Olé," he said. "My name is Devon, and I'll be your waiter tonight. Would you like to hear our specials?"

"Very professional," Bess said.

Devon took a bow. "Thank you."

"I don't need to hear the specials. I'll have the Tierra del Fuego burger," Bess said.

"And you'll want at least five glasses of water with that." Devon made a note on his pad.

Bess looked worried. "Is it that spicy?"

Devon nodded. "And then some. The name means Land of Fire."

"Maybe I'll have what Marisa's having," Bess decided. "That would be—"

Devon waved his hand. "I already wrote it down. Tortilla soup, quesadilla, flan. Right?"

"Right," Nancy said. "And that's what I want, too."

"Me, too." George closed her menu. "That was easy, wasn't it?"

"I'll say." Devon took their menus. "I'll be right back with your soups."

A few minutes later, everyone was enjoying the tangy tomato, chicken broth, and tortilla mixture that Devon had set before them.

"It's hard to hold Casey's leash and eat at the same time," Bess said.

"You can try looping the end around your chair leg," Marisa suggested.

"Good idea." Bess stood and lifted her chair. The door to the kitchen opened, and Devon exited with two trays of Tierra del Fuego burgers, hot sauce, and several glasses of water.

Casey wagged her tail and ran to greet Devon.

Before Bess could stop her, the leash was tangled around Devon's feet.

"Whoa!" Devon shouted. He tried frantically to balance the slipping trays, but he could not. Glass shattered, and burgers and water rained down on the floor.

The restaurant grew silent. Bess's face turned as pink as their tablecloth. "I am so sorry." She scooped Casey into her lap and checked her paws for cuts.

Devon looked at the mess around him, then burst out laughing. "Well, I've never done *that* before."

"Is everyone all right?" Marisa asked.

Once he was certain no one had been hurt, Devon hurried into the kitchen for a broom, dustpan, and mop.

"Let me help you," Bess said when Devon returned.

Devon smiled. "That's okay. I think you have your hands full watching Casey."

Eric and his friends also came over and offered to help.

"Thanks, guys, but I've got it under control," Devon said. A waitress and a busboy came from the kitchen, each holding a broom. "Great. Reinforcements."

Amber passed by the table on her way to the ladies' room. She shook her finger at Casey. "Is this any way to behave in a restaurant?" She giggled. "When does she start obedience school, Bess?"

"Not soon enough," Bess said.

Mr. Marshall hurried after Amber. He took her by the shoulder and gently guided her away from the area that still had shards of glass on the floor. "Careful, Amber. Walk this way. You don't want to cut yourself." Amber followed her father on a roundabout route toward the rest rooms.

In less than five minutes the area was sparkling and fresh Tierra del Fuego burgers were sizzling on the grill.

George elbowed Bess. "What did your puppy book say about situations like this one?"

Bess frowned. "Nothing. Thank goodness Devon was so understanding."

"I told you he's a great waiter," Marisa said. "He's had customers scream at him, return their dinners several times, then refuse to pay him. Trust me, this was not a big deal."

"That's right," Devon said as he brought everyone's entrees. "So don't give it another thought . . . until it's time to calculate the tip, that is," he added with a grin.

George took a forkful of her Spanish rice. "This is delicious."

"Oops." Marisa set down her water.

"What?" Bess asked.

"I had my napkin in my lap, and I must have dropped it on the floor," Marisa said.

"I don't think so," George said, grabbing Casey by her collar. Marisa's pink napkin was clenched tightly in the puppy's teeth. Casey broke free and ran over to Nancy, who held her still while George and Bess extracted the napkin from the puppy's mouth. Marisa held Casey's leash while they all trooped to the bathroom to wash their hands.

"I hope our food's not cold," Bess said when they returned.

"Me, too," Nancy said. "I haven't even tasted it yet."

Marisa picked up her fork and carefully rested it on her food. "Rice," she murmured. "I can tell food by touch."

Nancy watched with interest as Marisa moved her fork clockwise. "And this must be the refried beans." She frowned.

"What's wrong?" Bess asked.

"Don't touch your food," Marisa said sharply.

Nancy stopped her fork on the way to her mouth. She gasped as she looked closely at the food. Her meal had been garnished with broken glass.

6

A Bark in the Dark

Nancy let her fork clatter to her plate. "Thank you, Marisa."

"What's the matter?" Bess asked.

"My meal is full of tiny pieces of broken glass," Nancy said.

Bess squinted at her food. "Mine seems fine."

"So does mine," George said.

Marisa sifted through her food with her fork. "I could feel there was something here that didn't belong. I didn't realize it was broken glass." She shuddered.

Nancy motioned for Devon and quietly explained to him what had happened. Before she finished three sentences, he hurried into the kitchen and got the manager.

Within minutes, the manager was announcing

to the diners that the restaurant had been closed for the night. He offered full refunds to all the diners, and rain checks to come again on other nights.

As the other patrons filed out, Devon pulled up a chair and sat next to Marisa.

"Did any of the other customers find glass in their meals?" Nancy asked him.

"No," Devon said. "But the manager's not sure how this happened, and we'd rather be safe than sorry. I'm sure it had something to do with this counterfeiting business," he added. "Somebody's trying to scare you two off the case again."

"That's certainly possible," Nancy said. "If this was done deliberately, the glass was added to our meals *after* you brought them to our table."

"Why do you say that?" Bess asked.

"Because we all ordered the same thing," Nancy explained. "There was no way to tell the difference between our meals until they were served."

"You and Bess and I went to the ladies' room," George said.

"I heard several people pass by our table while you were gone," Marisa said. "I didn't notice anything unusual, but it was noisy in here. Somebody certainly could have slipped the glass into the food then."

"Almost all the kitchen workers and waiters here are Westmoor students," Devon said. "Not to mention the people who eat here. And don't the police think the person responsible for circulating the counterfeit money is a Westmoor student?"

"Probably," Nancy said. "I also understand that a lot of counterfeit money has shown up at Café Olé. But I don't suppose any of the waiters has been a Westmoor student for, say, twenty-five years?"

Devon chuckled. "I don't think so. We're all more or less the same age."

"Any more ideas?" Nancy asked Devon.

"No." Devon took Marisa's hand. "Marisa, please tell me you'll give up this investigation. I don't want anything to happen to you."

Marisa squeezed his hand. "Nothing will happen to me."

Devon shook his head. "I can't believe you'd put yourself in this much danger for Eric. I know he's your friend, but I don't like him, I don't trust him, and—"

"Devon," Marisa said gently, "Eric *is* my friend, and I *do* want to clear his name. But even more important, I want to protect my grandmother's reputation and the future of Candlelight Inn. Until we learn who hid the old counterfeit money there, people will always wonder."

The manager beckoned to Devon. "I'd better go back to work," Devon told the group.

"When will you be home?" Marisa asked.

"I'm scheduled to close," Devon explained. "We're going to do a safety check, then I have to mop my station. I think it'll be a few more hours, at least."

"Okay," Marisa said. She leaned over to kiss his cheek. "I'll see you tomorrow."

"Is that your stomach growling, or Casey?" George asked Bess as they exited the restaurant.

Bess pressed her hand against her stomach. "Sorry. I'm starving."

"There's a hot dog and burger place across the street," Marisa said. "Top Dog. It's pretty good. Do you want to stop there?"

"Great idea," Nancy said, and Bess and George agreed.

"Top Dog. We like the name, don't we, Casey?" Bess patted Casey's head.

Inside the restaurant, Bess quietly read the menu to Marisa, then everyone placed their orders.

At the register, the cashier handed Marisa several bills in change. Marisa pulled a small, rectangular device from her pocket and inserted the bills into it one at a time. "Five dollars," a computerized voice pronounced as Marisa inserted the first bill. Marisa folded it in half and inserted the next bill. "One dollar." Marisa folded down the opposite corners of the one-dollar bill.

"That's a great way to keep track of your money," Nancy said.

Marisa nodded. "Coins are easy to tell apart by touch, but paper money is impossible because it's all the same size. Without this device and a good system, I'd be lost. I used to have a wallet with lots of compartments, but when we were dating, Eric taught me this system of folding the money. I find it much simpler."

Nancy whisked her tray from the counter and took a sip of her thick milk shake. "You and Eric used to date?" That would explain the bad vibes between Devon and Eric, she thought.

They took seats at a booth. "Devon hates the fact that Eric and I are still friends," Marisa said. "He won't come out and say it—I mean, he and Eric are fraternity brothers. Still, I'm sure he'd be happy if Eric fell off the face of the earth." Marisa sighed.

"Devon loves you," Bess said.

Marisa smiled. "I know. And I love him. I only wish he trusted me a little more. Eric and I are friends, and that's all. Why is that so hard for Devon to understand?"

Bess put a hand on Marisa's shoulder. "Who knows? Men are hard to figure."

"You can say that again." Marisa bit off the end of a french fry. Casey rested her chin on George's shoe and looked up at her with a pitiful expression in her eyes.

"Bess," George said, "may I please give her a french fry?"

"Absolutely not." Bess tugged on Casey's leash. "The first thing Penny told me was no table food. A couple of french fries, and she'll be a guide dog has-been. Besides, fries aren't good for dogs."

"Or for people," George said.

Bess bit her lip. "I know. But they taste so good. How can you sit here and eat a salad with all these yummy, fattening foods surrounding you?"

"I have a race tomorrow," George said. "Remember?"

"You have to be up early, don't you?" Nancy asked. "Five o'clock."

"You're not waking me up at five again, are you, Casey?" Bess yawned as she patted the puppy's head.

Marisa wiped off her greasy fingers and touched them to her Braille watch face. "It's nine o'clock already?"

"Do you need to get home?" Bess asked.

"I do have a lot of homework tonight," Marisa said.

George stood up. "I definitely need a good night's sleep. I'll take you home, Marisa."

"Thanks." Marisa said good night to Nancy and Bess.

Nancy and Bess stayed at the restaurant for

69

coffee, then headed home. Nancy shivered as she and Bess walked back to her car. "It really is chilly."

Bess bent down and hugged Casey. "Are you cold, Casey? Maybe I'll use Marisa's sewing machine to make you some warm clothes."

Nancy chuckled. "You've got to be kidding."

"I guess Casey does have a built-in fur coat," Bess said. "I'm just anxious to sew something, and I wanted to start out simple."

"Dog clothes do not sound simple to me," Nancy said.

"You're probably right." Bess tugged lightly on Casey's leash. "I still can't believe Marisa gave me her sewing machine. I hope things work out for her and Devon."

"Me, too," Nancy said as they reached her car.

"We'll sit in the back so Casey has plenty of room," Bess said when Nancy had unlocked the door on the passenger side. She lifted Casey onto the backseat and climbed in after her.

"Did you know that Devon proposed to Marisa a few weeks ago?" Bess asked as Nancy adjusted the driver's seat to give Bess and Casey more room in the back.

"No." Nancy turned the key in the ignition. "What happened?" She looked over her shoulder and backed out of the parking space.

"Marisa said no," Bess replied. "Devon told me. He was pretty upset. Marisa said she wanted to wait until they both graduated from school and their lives were more stable, but Devon's afraid—"

"I know what you're going to say," Nancy cut in. "Devon's afraid Marisa still has feelings for Eric."

"Exactly." Bess pulled Casey away from the seat belt. "Besides, Devon wants to be an actor. He's not sure his life will *ever* be stable."

"I thought he was in architecture school for that very reason," Nancy said. "Stability."

"He's in architecture school because his father wants him to be. He made that very clear at the inn. He's taking acting classes on the side because *he* wants to." Bess smiled. "We used to put on neighborhood plays all the time when we were growing up. Everyone wanted to be the hero except for Devon. He wanted to be the bad guy. That's when we all knew he was a serious actor." Bess giggled. "Once, he even got a black eye when he tried to kiss Laura Fissinger."

"I remember now. Didn't you fall off the stage and sprain your ankle during one of your productions?"

Bess frowned. "I can't believe you remember that."

When they arrived at Bess's house, Bess invited Nancy inside. "Would you like some hot chocolate?" Bess asked once they were in the kitchen.

"No, thanks. But I'll sit while you have a snack."

Bess set Casey down and washed her hands. "How about some chocolate chip cookies? I've been doing a lot of baking since my parents went away. It's fun to experiment when no one cares how messy the kitchen gets."

"No, thanks. We just ate, remember?"

They went into the living room, and Bess grabbed the remote control. "I wonder if there's anything good on TV tonight."

Nancy looked at her watch. "Bess, it's late. I should get home."

"Do you have to? Why don't you spend the night? Come on, Nan—it would be fun."

Nancy yawned. "I don't know. . . ."

"Please?" Bess's blue eyes were wide. "I hate being in this house alone at night. Casey barks at every little sound—it's creepy."

Casey leaped up and yapped ferociously. The hairs on the back of her neck stood up.

The doorbell rang. Bess glanced at Nancy. "See what I mean? Who'd be visiting at this hour?"

Bess stood on her tiptoes and timidly looked out the peephole of the front door. "George!" she exclaimed. She swung open the door.

George, Marisa, and Misty were standing on the front porch. "Hi again," George said. Bess showed them inside.

"What's the matter?" Nancy asked.

"My apartment was flooded tonight," Marisa said glumly. "A pipe burst—everything's a mess."

"Marisa needs a place to stay until the water damage is repaired," George explained. "And I thought you might like some company, Bess. . . ."

"You're right about that," Bess said. "Marisa, did George explain that my parents are out of town? I was just badgering Nancy into spending the night because I was so lonely. I'd be thrilled to have a temporary roommate."

"That's just what I thought you'd say. Marisa's bags are in my car," George said with a grin. "I'll bring them inside."

"Thanks, George," Marisa said. "And thank you, Bess. You're the best."

Misty licked Bess's hand. "I'm glad you're here, too, Misty," Bess said as she guided Casey away from an electrical cord. "Any tips on puppy-raising would be greatly appreciated."

"Do you mind if I use your phone?" Marisa asked. "I'm going to call Devon and let him know I'm staying here."

"Sure," Bess said. She turned to Nancy. "Are you still going to stay?"

Nancy smiled. "Why not? We can have a slumber party."

George entered with two small shoulder bags. Her smartly styled short hair was now a mass of dark, wet ringlets. "It's pouring outside," she said.

Thunder boomed and echoed in the distance. Casey barked and shivered against Bess's leg.

"I hope this doesn't last all night," Bess said as she led everyone upstairs and showed them to their rooms.

When she came downstairs in the morning, Nancy laughed. Bess's hair was tousled, and she had an exasperated expression on her face.

"Someone woke up on the wrong side of the bed this morning," Nancy said with a teasing expression.

"Easy for you to say," Bess said. "You weren't dragged outside four times in the driving rain in the middle of the night to wait for *ten minutes* for your dog to go to the bathroom."

"No," Nancy said, "but I *was* awakened at ten-minute intervals by your dog's barking with every clap of thunder."

Bess wagged her finger at Casey. "Misty was a nice, quiet dog. Why can't you be more like Misty?"

"Bess!" Marisa called from upstairs.

Reacting to the urgency in their friend's voice, Bess and Nancy hurried up to the guest bedroom. Marisa was sitting up in bed.

"Have you seen Misty?" she asked.

74

"No," Bess said. "She was sleeping on the floor next to your bed most of the night."

"I know," Marisa said. "But she's gone, and she didn't come when I called her."

Nancy and Bess walked through the house, whistling and calling Misty's name.

"It's no use," Marisa finally said. "She's gone. Someone stole Misty."

7

Muddy Pawprints

"I took Casey out several times last night," Bess said. "Maybe Misty slipped outside."

"No. She wouldn't leave me," Marisa insisted.

"Normally, I'm sure that's true," Nancy said, "but maybe with the unfamiliar surroundings and the thunderstorm . . ."

Marisa bit her lip. Tears glistened in her eyes. "She wouldn't leave me. I'm sure she was taken."

Nancy quickly got dressed and went outside. In the mud, she found small pawprints next to a large set of sneaker prints. She surmised that since the sneaker prints were much larger than Bess's, it seemed that Marisa was right. Misty must have been stolen.

"Did you leave the door unlocked when you

took Casey out?" Nancy asked Bess as she stepped inside.

Bess shook her head. "I'm sure I didn't. I was careful because of the threats against you and Marisa."

When she examined the Marvins' locks, Nancy found no sign of forced entry. "It's just like the break-in at your apartment," she told Marisa. "It doesn't make sense."

Marisa shakily set down the glass of orange juice Bess had poured for her. "What if something happened to Misty? What am I going to do?"

Bess looked as though she might cry, too. "I'm so sorry, Marisa."

"How can I go to class?" Marisa bit her thumbnail fiercely. "Not only will I not be able to concentrate, but I won't be able to find my way around. I never learned how to use a cane very well. And I'm not even staying in my own apartment. I'll never be able to manage."

"What can we do to help?" Nancy asked.

"Could you bring me the phone?" Marisa asked. "I'm going to call Devon."

"We'll give you some privacy," Nancy said. She and Bess took Casey to the kitchen.

"Do you think Misty's disappearance is related to the counterfeiting case?" Bess asked Nancy.

Nancy shrugged. "A well-trained guide dog is worth a lot of money, right?"

Bess nodded. "Several thousand dollars."

"It could be theft, plain and simple," Nancy said. "Then again, what better way to sideline Marisa than to take Misty? But who knew Marisa was staying here? And how did the thief get in?"

Bess patted Casey's head. "You probably tried to warn us last night, and we thought you were barking at the thunder."

"Bess?" Marisa called from the living room.

Bess held open the swinging door for Nancy and Casey. "What's going on?" she asked Marisa.

Marisa drew in a deep breath. "Well, Devon said that between his work hours and the fall play, he's too busy to give me much extra help, but Eric promised to make sure I get from class to class."

Bess and Nancy exchanged a look. Devon was too busy to help Marisa at a time like this? That seemed terribly insensitive, Nancy thought. Besides, wasn't the restaurant still closed following last night's incident with the broken glass?

Marisa shifted in her seat. "Nancy, could I ask you a huge favor?"

"Sure," Nancy said.

"Could you give me a ride to the inn? I promised I'd meet Penny this morning, and we're not on the bus line here."

"Not a problem," Nancy said. "Anyhow, I was hoping to talk to Penny and learn a little more about the history of the inn. I figure any extra information might help with the counterfeiting case."

Marisa nodded. "You could be right. But I doubt Penny knows more than what I've already told you about the inn. I certainly don't."

"Okay," Nancy said. "In that case, maybe I'll try the River Heights Historical Society. But, I'll still take you to the inn, of course."

After dropping off Marisa, Nancy drove to the historical society, in downtown River Heights. A tall, thin woman sat behind a glass case in the empty reception area. The case was filled with old china, buttons, maps, money, and even a copper dustpan.

The woman stood up and shook Nancy's hand. "Hi. I'm Betsy Lesh, president of the historical society. Have you seen our display of nineteenth-century household items?" She gestured toward the glass case. "These items are replicas, of course—the originals are very valuable to collectors. Perhaps you'd like to visit the recently restored Sorensen home on Main Street to experience a typical River Heights home of the time period."

"That sounds interesting," Nancy said. "Maybe another time."

"How may I help you today?" Betsy asked.

Nancy explained that she was looking for information about the history of Candlelight Inn.

Betsy's eyes lit up as Nancy spoke. "I have a

wonderful book here on Illinois inns and taverns that dedicates several pages to Candlelight Inn." She scanned the bookshelf behind her. "Here it is. Have you seen this?" she asked Nancy as she took the book off the shelf.

Nancy shook her head.

"It's really quite fascinating," Betsy said. She ran her finger down the table of contents, turned to a page, then began to read aloud. " 'The inn was built in 1853 by Edward Allen Taper, a self-made millionaire.' "

Betsy looked up from the book. "Not that it says so here, but he was rumored to be a stingy old man. Stingy but brilliant. Much of his fortune disappeared over the years, but the inn still stands as a legacy of his vision. I'm sure you've read about Emmaline Whitby in the newspapers, and her bequest to the Guiding Eyes?"

Nancy nodded.

"Obviously, Emmaline inherited her great-grandfather's financial talents," Betsy said. "But unlike Edward Taper, she was a truly generous individual who made numerous charitable contributions. Of course, we at the Society would have been happier had she not undertaken those extensive renovations at the inn thirty years ago, when she converted it to a full-time residence. Nonetheless, much of the original structure remains intact."

"I took a tour of the inn recently," Nancy said. "The construction is beautiful."

Betsy nodded. "And the renovations were performed by Marshall and Marshall. They did an excellent job, and took great care to restore and preserve what they could."

"Marshall?" Nancy repeated. "As in Larry Marshall?"

"That's right," Betsy said. "Larry Marshall and his father, Tom. I understand that Larry's son, Devon, is following the family tradition and going to architecture school. If he's as talented as his father, he has quite a future. It's a shame Larry's business has fallen on hard times. Between the poor real estate market and Emmaline's will . . ."

"Emmaline's will? Was Mr. Marshall expecting to receive an inheritance?" Nancy asked.

Betsy laughed. "Oh, my, no. I don't think so. But he did hope to purchase Candlelight Inn after Emmaline's death. He wanted to make it the cornerstone of a fully restored, historic shopping district. He's been planning this for years. Unfortunately, because Emmaline bequeathed the inn to the Guiding Eyes, Mr. Marshall's plans will never be realized." Betsy sighed. "We at the historical society are quite disappointed. Of course, we think the Guiding Eyes school is a wonderful project, too."

"Yes," Nancy said. "Thank you for your help."

"It was a pleasure, dear." Betsy Lesh smiled. "May I help you with anything else? A walking tour of downtown River Heights, perhaps?"

"Definitely next time," Nancy said.

Nancy left with a handful of River Heights brochures. She looked at her watch. She'd been so engrossed in what Betsy Lesh was telling her that she'd lost track of time.

Nancy's mind raced as she drove to the inn. Now she knew that Mr. Marshall had had access to the inn many years before. Since he and his father did the renovations, surely he must have known about the hidden room. And he had been at the restaurant the night of the broken glass incident. Could he be the counterfeiter?

Nancy turned into the driveway at the inn and was surprised to see three police cars parked under the apple trees. Penny and Marisa stood on the front lawn.

Nancy quickly parked and hopped out of her car. "What's going on?" she asked Marisa.

"Nancy, I'm glad you're here," Marisa said. "On top of everything that's been happening, now the inn's been vandalized!"

8

Where There's a Will, There's a Way

"Marisa and I drove to Westmoor for lunch," Penny said. "When we got back, the inn was a shambles. Drawers were pulled out and overturned. Paintings were slashed. There's even some structural damage to the building."

Nancy saw that a hollow in a giant oak tree near the house had been enlarged with an ax or a saw. Sap oozed from the gaping hole. "That poor old tree is going to die," she said. "Why would anyone do such a terrible thing?"

"I don't know." Marisa shivered. "Do you think it's safe to go inside now?"

Detective Lee and another police officer came out of the house and approached Marisa. "Ms. Henares, forensics has finished collecting evidence. We'll be in touch as soon as we learn anything."

"Detective Lee, do you think this sabotage is related to the counterfeiting case?" Nancy asked.

"We don't have enough information at this time to answer that question," Lee replied. "Right now, we're treating it as a separate matter."

After the police had left, Nancy and Penny guided Marisa back up the hill to the inn.

"What's going on, Nancy?" Marisa asked. "Why would someone do this?"

"I don't know," Nancy said. "If it was the counterfeiter, maybe he or she was trying to destroy evidence—or was looking for more hidden money."

Penny swept up broken glass from under Emmaline's portrait in the study. "What a mess," she said.

Marisa began to gather her grandmother's papers from the floor and put them back in order.

"Let me help you," Penny said.

Marisa shook her head. "That's okay. I've got a system here. I need to do this myself."

Penny leaned on the broom. "I don't know what the Guiding Eyes people are going to say when they hear about this. The finances for the school were already tight. With all this damage . . . I really don't know how we're going to pull off this project."

"What about the insurance?" Marisa asked.

"That will help," Penny said. "But we're still responsible for paying part of the cost of the damage, which is a lot of money."

"Where there's a will, there's a way," Marisa said.

Penny sighed. "I hope so, Marisa."

Marisa touched her watch. "I have to get to class." She shoved her grandmother's papers into her briefcase. "Don't work too hard, Penny. I'll be back later to help."

Nancy gave Marisa a ride to campus and made arrangements to pick her up in an hour and a half.

When she returned home, Carson Drew was sitting down to a late lunch in the dining room. A thick volume lay open next to a glass of iced tea.

"Have you eaten yet?" he asked Nancy.

Nancy shook her head. "It's been a hectic morning." She sat down at the table and told her father about the break-in at Candlelight Inn.

"Hmm . . ." Mr. Drew said.

Nancy's blue eyes twinkled. "Hmm?" she repeated. "Any hunches?"

Mr. Drew nodded. "As a matter of fact, yes. Anyone interested in contesting the terms of Emmaline's will might benefit from extensive damage to the inn. If the Guiding Eyes can't establish the school in River Heights, other potential heirs could say that Emmaline's wishes aren't being followed. Then they could argue that the money should go to them instead."

Nancy nodded thoughtfully. "That's a good point, Dad. But Marisa is Mrs. Whitby's only living relative, so I don't think there *are* any other potential heirs. Wait a minute," she said after a moment. "There is Larry Marshall."

Mr. Drew blinked. "Devon and Amber's father? Is he a relative?"

Nancy shook her head. "No, but I just learned today that he was hoping to save his land developing business by turning Candlelight Inn into part of a historic shopping district. If the inn was available, he'd probably be the first in line to buy it."

Mr. Drew speared a lettuce leaf with his fork. "Interesting theory."

"Then there are the Guiding Eyes people," Nancy said. "The organization will get some insurance money because of the damage. And Penny Rosen has mentioned a few times that they'd like to drop the Candlelight Inn renovation and use the money somewhere else. But according to the terms of Mrs. Whitby's will, that's not possible—is it?"

"If they agreed to take Emmaline's money to build the school, they're pretty much stuck," Mr. Drew said, "unless there are extenuating circumstances."

"Like major damage to the inn that no one could have foreseen?" Nancy asked.

Mr. Drew set down his fork. "Are you saying the Guiding Eyes may have sabotaged the project to make Emmaline's money available for other needs?"

Nancy sighed. "I guess that's what I'm saying. I mean, it's possible, isn't it? Anything's possible."

Mr. Drew nodded. "You can say that again."

"I'm going to see Marisa this afternoon," Nancy said. "She's been through so much these past few days—I don't know if I have the heart to suggest that Devon's father and the Guiding Eyes are the chief suspects so far."

"Play it by ear," Mr. Drew suggested. "That's what I intend to do with Judge Medina this afternoon. Everything depends on how his golf game went this morning."

"Probably not well," Nancy said. "Have you seen the mud?"

Mr. Drew put down his napkin and stood up from the table. "You have a point there. This should be an interesting afternoon for both of us."

After her father left, Nancy quickly ate a sandwich and drove back to the university to pick up Marisa.

"How was class?" Nancy asked as she guided Marisa toward the Mustang.

Marisa shrugged. "I didn't have my reading finished—and of course the professor called on me." Marisa closed her eyes. "A lot of people asked about Misty. It's been a rough day."

87

Nancy's heart went out to Marisa. Her friend seemed exhausted. Nancy decided that this was not a good time to discuss her latest theories in the counterfeiting case, and she kept the conversation going with light chatter during the drive to the Marvin home.

Bess had a tray of warm peanut butter cookies waiting for Marisa and Nancy in the kitchen when they arrived.

"Do dogs like peanut butter?" Bess asked Marisa. "Casey's been begging for a taste all day."

Marisa laughed. "I've never met a dog that didn't like peanut butter. Don't give in, though—it's very fattening."

The doorbell rang. Casey yapped and dashed to the foyer. Bess followed and opened the door. "Hi, Amber."

Amber skipped inside. "Hi. May I take Casey for a walk?"

"Of course you may," Bess said. "Thanks for the help."

Amber took off her coat and leaned over to pet Casey. Casey's tail wagged as she sniffed Amber's sweater. Slowly, she circled Amber, her black nose twitching.

"What do you smell, Casey?" Bess asked.

"I just had an ice cream cone," Amber said. "Does she like ice cream?"

"Probably," Bess said. "Maybe you spilled some on your sweater." Casey sneezed, and Bess leaned over to pick her up. She looked closely at Amber's sweater.

"Did I spill anything?" Amber asked.

"What?" Bess distractedly put Casey down again.

"Did I spill ice cream on my sweater?" Amber repeated.

"Oh—no, you didn't," Bess said. "Are you ready to go?"

"Come on, Casey. Do you want to go for a walk?" Amber pulled on her coat again as Nancy and Marisa came into the foyer.

"Why don't you go, too, Marisa?" Bess suggested.

"Good idea," Marisa said. "I can use a break from studying."

As soon as the door closed behind the dog-walkers, Nancy turned to Bess. "What was that all about?"

"Was I that obvious?" Bess asked.

"No, but I know you," Nancy said. "You wanted to get Marisa out of here. What's going on?"

"When I was picking up Casey, I saw hairs on Amber's sweater. Short, black hairs." Bess took a deep breath before she continued. "They certainly weren't Amber's. Amber has light hair. I think the dark hairs belonged to Misty."

9

A Hairy Problem

"No wonder Casey was so interested in Amber's sweater—she smelled Misty." Nancy followed Bess back to the kitchen. "The Marshalls have a spare key to your house, don't they?"

Bess nodded. "For general emergencies. Plus, they water our plants when we go on vacation."

"I know Amber's anxious to have a dog of her own," Nancy said. "Do you think—"

"No," Bess said firmly. "Amber loves Misty, but she also loves Marisa. I'm sure she wouldn't steal Misty."

"What about Devon?" Nancy asked.

"Devon? Why would *he* take Misty?" Bess asked.

Nancy paused for a moment. "What if Devon's involved in passing the counterfeit money?"

Bess shook her head. "No way."

"Devon's father worked on the renovations at the inn," Nancy said. "So, Mr. Marshall must have known about the hidden room where we found the counterfeit money. Maybe Devon knew, too. And since he and Eric are fraternity brothers, this could be how Eric got involved in this whole mess."

"Wait a minute," Bess said. "Devon and Eric can't stand each other."

"That's right," Nancy said. "What if Devon framed Eric?"

Bess's mouth dropped open. "What?"

"Devon hates the fact that Marisa and Eric are friends. If Eric were in jail, that would solve at least one of Devon's problems."

"But Eric's *not* in jail," Bess said. "And if anything, Marisa's spent extra time with him, trying to clear his name. She's been working hard on the counterfeiting case."

Nancy nodded. "I know. But hear me out. Maybe Devon didn't realize Marisa would get so involved. And maybe that's why he decided to steal Misty—to stop Marisa before she figured out he was involved in the case."

"That would explain why Devon wouldn't help Marisa after Misty was taken." Bess sighed. "This is depressing. I've always liked Devon. I can't believe he's the counterfeiter."

"He's too young to be the counterfeiter," Nancy said. "I'm just saying he might have known about the phony money at the inn, and he might have given some of that money to Eric, hoping that Eric would get caught spending it. Devon lives at home, so he could have used the spare key to your house to steal Misty. He knew Marisa was staying here after the flood at her apartment, because she called him. And he certainly had the best access to our dishes at the restaurant last night. He could easily have added the glass to our meals after Casey made him drop the tray."

"But what if those *weren't* Misty's hairs on Amber's sweater?" Bess asked.

Nancy shrugged. "Then I'm probably wrong."

"We could go over to the Marshalls' yard and check for pawprints," Bess suggested. "If Devon has Misty, he can't keep her in the house all day. Believe me."

"Good idea." Nancy went to the closet for her coat. "With all this mud, there would be prints. Let's hurry before Amber and Marisa come back."

The doorbell rang.

"I'll get it," Nancy said. She opened the door, and Misty's big, muddy paws nearly knocked her over. Devon yanked on her leash.

Nancy locked eyes with Devon while Misty strained on her leash, eager to find Marisa.

"Please don't ask any questions. Is Marisa here?" Devon asked.

Nancy shook her head. "She and Amber are walking Casey. They'll be back soon."

"May I come in?"

Nancy stepped aside. "I guess so."

Devon sat silently on the couch and absent-mindedly petted Misty until Marisa and Amber returned with Casey. Casey let out an excited yelp and ran to greet Misty.

"Misty!" Amber shouted. "Devon, you found her!" She threw her arms around the dog. With a polite wag of the tail, Misty wriggled away and ran to Marisa. Marisa knelt on the floor, and Misty licked away her tears. "I love you, Misty," Marisa whispered. "Please be okay."

"She's fine," Devon said. His voice quavered slightly.

Marisa put her arm around him. "What happened? What's wrong?"

"I don't know how to tell you this, Marisa. I made a huge mistake." Devon took a deep breath. "I took Misty."

Marisa's hand clenched. "You what?"

"It was a terrible thing to do. I don't know what I was thinking." Devon ran his hands through his hair. "I wasn't thinking. I was so worried about you. The only way I could imagine keeping you out of danger was to force you to give up this case."

"By taking Misty?" Marisa backed away from Devon. "You really thought that would work?"

93

"I told you," Devon said, "I wasn't thinking. I was afraid of what might happen to you. Someone has threatened your life. Why do you have to be so stubborn?"

"Don't try to blame this on me," Marisa said angrily, then softened. "Why did you change your mind? Why did you bring Misty back?"

"Because you're obviously determined to keep working on the counterfeiting case," Devon said. "We were all miserable. I had to hide Misty in the basement, and she cried all day long. She would have given herself away sooner or later."

"I thought I heard something when we were doing the laundry," Amber said. "You told me it was the washing machine making a funny noise."

"Sorry, Amber." Devon looked down at the floor.

Bess pointed to Amber's sweater. "Dog hair gets everywhere, you know."

Devon looked surprised when he saw Misty's black hairs clinging to Amber's sweater. "You must have rubbed against some of my clothes while we were doing the laundry, Amber." He turned to Bess and Nancy. "You knew?"

Bess nodded. "We just figured it out. *I* couldn't believe you'd take Misty. Nancy had to convince me."

Nancy averted her eyes. She was glad Bess hadn't mentioned her suspicions that Devon could be involved in passing the counterfeit money. Even if Devon was telling the truth about his reasons for taking Misty, he was still a lead suspect. He had the means, the motive, and the opportunity, Nancy thought. And as a drama student he could probably put on a convincing act for all of them.

"Will you forgive me?" Devon asked Marisa.

"I know you love me, Devon. And I love you." Marisa scratched Misty behind the ears. "But my head is spinning right now. I don't know if I can forgive you. Please give me some time to think."

"Okay." Devon stood. "Come on, Amber. Let's go home."

Amber pulled her mittens out of her pocket, and Casey tried to snatch one.

"No, Casey. We're not playing now." Amber waved solemnly at Nancy and Bess. "'Bye."

After Amber and Devon left, Bess sat next to Marisa on the sofa. "Is there anything I can get you?"

"No, thanks. I think I'm just going to sit here for a few minutes."

"We'll give you some privacy," Bess said.

Nancy climbed the stairs ahead of Bess. "Where's Casey?" she asked.

"Uh-oh." Bess darted around Nancy and ran up the rest of the stairs. "Casey?" she called. "I'm sure she's up to something."

"There she is," Nancy said as Casey darted out

of the guest bedroom where Marisa had been sleeping and into Bess's bedroom.

Bess raced after her. "She has something in her mouth."

Nancy laughed. "How can you tell?"

"She has that guilty look." Bess chased Casey and tried to pull her out from underneath the bed. "I hope Marisa didn't leave anything valuable lying around."

Nancy pried open Casey's jaws and held them while Bess fished out shredded pieces of green paper.

"Oh, no," Bess said. "Money." She turned to Casey. "Bad girl, Casey. Bad."

Casey tucked her tail between her legs and hung her head. Bess arranged several pieces of the shredded bill on her palm until she found a corner. "A twenty-dollar bill," she announced. "You would have expensive taste, Casey."

"Just like you," Nancy said, laughing.

Bess found a plastic bag and dropped the soggy pieces into it. "I guess I'll take this to the bank. If they can piece it together, do you think they'll believe what happened and give me a new one?"

"I'm sure this kind of thing happens all the time," Nancy said.

Bess sighed. "I'll bet Misty never behaved like this. Let's not tell Marisa, okay?"

* * *

Half an hour later, Nancy nudged Bess forward toward the teller window at the bank. Bess held up her plastic bag. "Well—" she began.

"Teething puppy?" the teller asked.

Bess smiled with relief. "How did you know?"

"Happens all the time," the teller replied. "Hang on a second, and I'll bring you a brand-new bill."

The teller took a few pieces from the bag and examined them. Then she went to the back of the bank.

"Why can't she just open up her money drawer and give me a twenty?" Bess asked.

Nancy shrugged. "I guess they have a certain procedure to follow."

Bess saw the teller talking to a manager. "She has to ask the manager?"

The manager picked up the phone. Bess sighed. "Why is this taking so long?"

Bess jumped when she felt someone tap her on the shoulder. She whirled around to see two security guards. One of them took her arm. "Please come with me, miss." He began to lead her away from the teller's window.

Bess yanked away her arm. "Excuse me. What's going on?"

"As if you don't know," the guard said. "Your twenty-dollar bill is counterfeit. And you're in big trouble."

10

Arresting Evidence

"Counterfeit?" Bess turned to Nancy. "How can that be?"

The second security guard studied Nancy's face. "You look familiar. Wait a minute—aren't you the detective? Nancy something?"

"Nancy Drew."

The guard pointed at his name badge. "Bob Rusnak. And this is John Wyar."

Instead of saying hello, Wyar looked at Rusnak. "Detective? Give me a break. She's a teenager." Then he grabbed Bess by the arm again.

Bess's face was white. "Nancy," she whispered, "do something."

"If you'll excuse me, I'm going to call my father," Nancy told Rusnak. "He's an attorney."

"You do that," John said. "I'm going to call the police."

"Why don't you ask for Detective Lee?" Nancy pulled his number from her wallet. "He's handling the counterfeiting case. He'll tell you that I'm assisting the police in their investigation."

Wyar rolled his eyes. "Yeah, right."

Half an hour later, Nancy, Bess, and the security guards sat in the bank manager's office with Carson Drew and Detective Lee.

"You say the twenty-dollar bill was in your house?" Detective Lee asked Bess.

Bess looked at Nancy. "Yes."

"And you have no idea how it got there?"

Bess shook her head. "No, I honestly don't."

Mr. Drew cleared his throat. "Do you think Nancy and Bess would knowingly bring a counterfeit bill to the bank for replacement?"

"Of course not," Detective Lee said. "They're not suspects. I'm just trying to ascertain what happened."

"We'd like to find out, too," Nancy said.

Detective Lee stood. "You're free to go. But please call me if you have any sudden flashes of insight."

Nancy nodded. "You can be sure we will."

"By the way," Detective Lee said, "we were finally able to locate our files in storage on the twenty-five-year-old counterfeiting case. You're

99

welcome to come down to the station and take a look at them if you'd like."

"Thanks," Nancy said. "I'll call to arrange a time."

Mr. Drew walked Bess and Nancy to Nancy's car.

"Thanks, Mr. Drew," Bess said. "You're a life-saver. I haven't been so humiliated since—"

"Since yesterday, when Casey tripped Devon and made him drop a tray full of hamburgers and all those glasses of water," Nancy said.

Bess shook her head and gave Nancy and Mr. Drew a weak smile. "What a week."

"You have no idea where you got that counterfeit bill, Bess?" Mr. Drew asked.

"Not exactly," Bess said. "Casey took it from the guest bedroom, where Marisa's staying. I have no idea where *Marisa* got it."

"But we plan to ask her as soon as we get back to Bess's house," Nancy said.

"The counterfeit money was Marisa's?" Mr. Drew turned to Nancy. "Why didn't you tell Detective Lee that?"

"Because we didn't want to make things more complicated than they already are," Nancy said, unlocking the car doors.

"I consider Marisa a good friend, and I think Nancy does, too." Bess opened her door. "We want to ask her about it ourselves."

"If Marisa's involved in this counterfeiting

ring, she can forget about becoming a lawyer," Mr. Drew said. "The state bar does not look kindly upon attorneys with criminal records."

Nancy sighed. "I know. Marisa's no criminal. At least I hope she isn't."

"How did I wind up with a counterfeit bill?" Marisa said, shaking her head. She was seated on Bess's sofa, and Bess and Nancy had just finished explaining what had happened. "I'm sorry, Bess. I can't believe you were almost arrested because of me."

"It wasn't your fault," Bess said.

Marisa bit her lip. "I've been to Café Olé and the campus bookstore hundreds of times. Maybe I got the money at the same place Eric did. I don't know."

Nancy nodded. She could only imagine how often money exchanged hands on a college campus. Marisa could have received the bill as change anywhere. Then Nancy remembered the adaptive device Marisa used to identify her paper money. Nancy wondered whether it would work on counterfeit money. If it didn't, Marisa's story didn't make sense. If she had received a counterfeit bill as change and her device wouldn't read it, Marisa would have known something was wrong.

Nancy watched Marisa smile as Casey tried to climb into her lap. Had she misjudged Marisa?

Nancy wondered. Could she be involved in passing the counterfeit money?

Nancy stood. "I'm going to call Detective Lee. Maybe I can go to the station now and look through the old counterfeiting files."

Nancy called the police station and arranged to meet Detective Lee in an hour. Then she went upstairs to the guest bedroom. She looked through Marisa's handbag until she found the money identifier. She tucked it into her pocket, with plans to return it later that night.

At the police station, Nancy found Detective Lee kicking the vending machine. "It won't take my dollar," he explained. Nancy pulled a crisp dollar from her pocket. "Let's trade."

"Thanks." Detective Lee inserted Nancy's bill into the machine and selected a chocolate marshmallow crispy bar. The red light on the machine began blinking, and no candy was delivered.

Detective Lee pressed the change return button. Still nothing happened. Detective Lee kicked the machine again. "This thing hates me," he said.

Nancy took Detective Lee's crinkled bill and inserted it into the money identifier. "One dollar," the device said.

"Wow," Detective Lee said. "That's amazing."

"It seems to work on money in poor condition." Nancy pocketed the bill. "I wonder whether it works on counterfeit money."

"Why do you need to know that?" Lee asked.

Nancy shrugged. "Just curious. Would you mind if I tried the device on some of the counterfeit bills you seized from the inn?"

"I don't see why not," Detective Lee said. "But I'll have to escort you to the evidence room."

"Lead the way," Nancy said.

Nancy followed Detective Lee through a maze of rooms on the first floor of the station house. Finally, they reached a room jammed full of everything from rusty tricycles to jewelry.

Detective Lee found a labeled plastic bag filled with money and brought it to Nancy. He put on a rubber glove and extracted one counterfeit twenty-dollar bill.

As Nancy held the device, Detective Lee inserted the money into it. "Error," the device said. Detective Lee tried another bill. "Error."

Nancy sighed. Her hunch was right. The device wouldn't read counterfeit money. Marisa was smart, and she knew all about the counterfeiting case, Nancy thought sadly. If Marisa had received the phony twenty-dollar bill as change, she should have had good reason to suspect it might be counterfeit.

"Okay," Detective Lee said. "Are you going to clue me in here? What does this mean?"

"I don't know yet," Nancy said quietly. "May I look at those old case files now?"

103

"Sure." Detective Lee led her back through the station to another room containing wall-to-wall filing cabinets. He wove through several rows until they reached a tall, gray cabinet near the back of the room. He knelt on the floor and opened the bottom drawer. "Half the files in this drawer pertain to the old counterfeiting case."

He stood up to make room for Nancy. "Have fun. I'll be at my desk if you need me."

Nancy thanked Detective Lee. After he left, she sat cross-legged on the floor with a file folder in her lap. It contained technical information regarding the production of the bills and a list of places where counterfeit money had been found twenty-five years earlier.

The second file folder described the arrests of Frank Goetz and Don Blevins for transporting the counterfeit money to Chicago. Goetz's work history included six months in the kitchen at Candlelight Inn before it was converted into Emmaline Whitby's private residence.

Blevins had been a gardener at several prominent River Heights homes. Nancy wondered whether he, too, had worked at Candlelight Inn. If the inn had been the headquarters of the counterfeiting ring, maybe this was how Goetz and Blevins had met their boss, Nancy figured.

In the third file folder, Nancy found a transcript of a police interrogation of a suspect in the case. She gasped when she saw the name of the suspect—Larry Marshall, Devon and Amber's father.

Nancy flipped through the rest of the documents in the file. Mr. Marshall had been arrested twenty-five years ago after passing several counterfeit bills at the Westmoor college dining hall. Like Eric, he was an architecture student with excellent drafting skills. He was considered the lead suspect, but there wasn't enough evidence to pursue the charges against him, so he was eventually released.

Nancy squinted at a notation written at the bottom of one of the pages of the document. When Mr. Marshall was arrested, his girlfriend had posted bail for him, the note said. Her name was Susan Whitby.

"Susan Whitby," Nancy whispered. "That's Marisa's mother."

11

A Handful of Suspects

Nancy's mind raced as she drove from the police station to Bess's house. She couldn't believe she hadn't made the connection sooner. Marisa was Emmaline Whitby's granddaughter. That made her the most obvious suspect of all.

Marisa had inherited Emmaline's furniture, but the Guiding Eyes got her fortune. What if Marisa wanted the money for herself? Nancy thought. Marisa was a law student. She must realize that if the plans to renovate the inn were sabotaged and the Guiding Eyes couldn't open the school, she would have a good chance of contesting her grandmother's will. And if Marisa was successful, she would get the money that Emmaline had left to the Guiding Eyes.

When she reached Bess's house, Nancy found

George and Bess playing on the floor with Casey. "How was the 5K race?" Nancy asked George.

"Except for all the mud, the race was pretty good," George said.

"Don't be so modest," Bess said. "She came in first in her age group."

"That's great!" Nancy said. She looked through her wallet for the money she had pledged to the Guiding Eyes and gave it to George.

"Thanks, Nan." George looked at Bess. "Marisa and Nancy are the only people who have paid me so far."

"I told you, I'm too embarrassed to show my face in the bank right now," Bess said. "I'll pay you in a few days, okay?"

George laughed. "Okay."

"Where's Marisa?" Nancy asked.

"She had a late class tonight." George threw Casey's tennis ball across the room, and Casey raced after it. "I dropped her off at the university."

"When will she be able to go back to her apartment?" Nancy asked Bess.

Casey nipped Bess's finger as Bess took the ball from her mouth. "Ow, Casey. Her landlord set up a couple of fans to dry out the carpets. They make a lot of noise, and Marisa is dependent on her sense of hearing, so she can't go back until at least tomorrow."

Nancy sat on the floor and crossed her legs. "I don't know if it's safe for Marisa to stay here alone with you tonight."

"We're not alone." Bess patted Casey's head. "We have two terrific watchdogs. And if the person passing the counterfeit money tries to get to Marisa again—"

"That's the problem," Nancy said. "I think *Marisa* may be involved in passing the counterfeit money."

Bess dropped the tennis ball. Casey grabbed it and ran across the room. "You're kidding."

"Have you ever known Nancy to kid about such a thing?" George asked Bess.

"What about all the threats against Marisa?" Bess asked.

"It's possible she engineered them herself," Nancy said. "Or maybe there are other people involved in passing the phony money who have it in for her."

"But why would Marisa work so hard to prove that Eric's not guilty? That doesn't make sense," Bess said.

"Of course it makes sense," George said. "In fact, it's brilliant. If she's the one who's guilty, who would suspect her?"

Bess crossed her arms. "You and Nancy would."

Briefly, Nancy explained what she had learned at the police station. "Susan Whitby was an artist—remember her portrait of Marisa's grandmother? We're looking for a talented forger, right? Marisa's mother could be the link between the old counterfeiting ring and the recent one."

"But Marisa's mother is dead," Bess said. "That's what Marisa told us."

George bounced the tennis ball. "She could have been lying."

"Even if Marisa's mother did die, she could have passed on to Marisa what she knew about the counterfeiting ring." Nancy turned to Bess. "Remember that mysterious feud between Marisa's mother and her grandmother?"

Bess nodded. "Marisa said they never spoke to each other again."

"Maybe they argued about the counterfeit money," Nancy said. She stood up. "Do you mind if I use your phone, Bess? And the phone book?"

"Of course not." Bess walked to the dining room and pulled out the phone book from a low shelf. "If you'd like to try to contact Susan Whitby, the number for the psychic hot line is in the front."

"Very funny." Nancy flipped through the book. "I'm calling Kay McNamara—Emmaline's housekeeper."

Within minutes Nancy had the answer she was looking for. She thanked Mrs. McNamara and hung up the phone. "Guess when Susan Whitby argued with her mother and left River Heights?"

"Twenty-five years ago," George said. "Bingo. It couldn't have been long after she posted bail for Devon's father."

Nancy returned the phone book to the shelf. "Tell me *that's* a coincidence, Bess."

"Okay," Bess said. "I have to admit—this is getting weird."

"Devon and his father, Marisa and her mother . . ." Nancy ticked off the names on her fingers. "It almost seems as if the counterfeiting ring was a family business, passed down from one generation to the next."

"What do you think we should do now?" Bess asked Nancy.

"I think we should confront Marisa with what we've learned and see what she says," Nancy replied.

George leaped to her feet. "Look at the time. I was supposed to pick up Marisa five minutes ago." She grabbed her keys and hurried out the door. "I'll be back in fifteen minutes."

"You look exhausted," Bess told Marisa when she came back with Misty and George.

"What a boring class." Marisa sank onto the sofa. "I *am* exhausted. Between working on my grandmother's will and studying, the counterfeiting case, and all this stress . . ." Marisa paused.

"Nancy, I don't know quite how to say this. What would you think if I decided not to pursue the case any further?"

"That's up to you, Marisa," Nancy said quietly.

"Well," Marisa said, "there don't seem to be any lingering suspicions about Eric. I talked to him tonight, and he wants me to give up the case. Anyhow, we're not making much progress. I just don't think it's worth it."

"But you were so determined before," Bess said.

"I know," Marisa said. "It's just that I have so much on my mind, and, besides, if Eric doesn't think I should work on the case, then why should I?"

"To prove that you're not the one passing the counterfeit money," Bess blurted out.

Marisa turned slowly toward Bess. "Excuse me?"

"Nancy went to the police and found out that Devon's father was charged in the counterfeiting case twenty-five years ago, and your mother bailed him out of jail." Bess's words ran together. "Then your mother argued with your grandmother and left town. All that money was found at the inn, and the inn was sabotaged, and . . ."

"And what does any of this have to do with me?" Marisa asked.

"Bess was almost arrested because you brought a counterfeit bill into her house," Nancy said.

"You claimed you didn't know the money was counterfeit, but I found out that your money identifier won't work on fake bills. Therefore, I think you knew better."

"I was wondering what happened to my money identifier," Marisa said.

"I borrowed it." Nancy reached into her pocket and handed it to Marisa. "We'd like an explanation, Marisa."

"You're right, Nancy. I do know something about the case that I haven't told you. Frankly, I'd rather not tell you now. But if you've pieced together this much, I'm sure you'll learn the truth soon enough."

Marisa took a deep breath. "I know who the counterfeiter is."

12

Truth or Snare?

"You're probably not going to believe this," Marisa began. "My grandmother was the head of the counterfeiting ring."

Bess's eyes widened. "Emmaline Whitby? That nice, sweet, old—"

"Blind lady?" Marisa finished for her. "Yes."

"But your grandmother died a couple of months ago—before any of the old counterfeit money resurfaced in River Heights," Nancy said.

Marisa nodded. "I know. I can't explain that—and I certainly didn't know the truth when I asked you to work on the case, Nancy."

"Are you sure about your grandmother's involvement?" Nancy asked Marisa.

"Oh, yes." Marisa leaned forward. "I never knew why my mother and grandmother were estranged. Neither one of them would talk about it. I found out this week when I was reading my grandmother's journal. Twenty-five years ago, Devon's father was dating my mother," Marisa explained. "I never knew that before." She paused.

"Go on," Nancy said gently. "I know this must be difficult for you."

"Somehow, Mr. Marshall accidentally came to possess some of my grandmother's counterfeit money. He was arrested when he tried to spend it, and he nearly went to jail. My mother was furious when she found out that my grand-mother—her own mother—was the counter-feiter."

"She had no idea?" George asked.

Marisa shook her head. "Apparently not. My grandmother was a very clever woman, you know." Marisa reached down to massage Misty's neck. "My mother loved my grandmother, but she couldn't forgive her. Still, she didn't want her own mother to go to jail. Rather than reveal the truth, my mother broke up with Devon's father, moved away from River Heights, and never talked to any of her friends or family again. She married my father, had me, and tried to forget the past."

Marisa bit her lip. "My grandmother was dev-astated to lose touch with her only child. She wrote her so many letters . . . but they were always returned unopened." Marisa's voice wavered.

Bess snatched a handful of tissues from the box in the kitchen. She gave some to Marisa and used one to dab at her own eyes.

"I assume your grandmother gave up counterfeiting for good?" Nancy said.

"Yes." Marisa blew her nose. "She wrote in her journal that becoming involved in the counterfeiting ring was her deepest regret in life. She felt responsible for the two men who were arrested when they were caught taking counterfeit money to Chicago. She supported their families while they were in jail, and then, after they were released, she gave them money for the rest of their lives. And she made charitable contributions to repay all the bad money. Even after she felt her debt was paid, she donated huge amounts of her money to worthy causes—like the Guiding Eyes. The Guiding Eyes school was her legacy to me. That's what she always told me."

Bess handed Marisa another tissue.

"I understand why my mother felt the way she did," Marisa said, "but I'm grateful that I got to spend time with my grandmother this past year. I grew to care for her very much. When I found out the truth, I only wanted to protect her."

"If your grandmother was so determined to change her life, I wonder why she left the counterfeit money in her house," Nancy said.

Marisa cleared her throat. "I don't know. Maybe she thought it was safer than trying to get rid of it. It would have been difficult after she lost her sight. Anyhow, she knew I'd learn the truth after she died. She left me her journal."

"And what about the counterfeit twenty-dollar bill that Casey found?" Nancy asked.

"It was with my grandmother's things," Marisa explained. "My money identifier wouldn't read it, and I figured it was probably counterfeit. I stuck it in my pocket and planned to get rid of it, but Casey beat me to it."

Marisa shook her head. "I can't believe I was so stupid. I almost got all of us in trouble. Now I understand why Mr. Marshall doesn't want me and Devon to date."

"What do you mean?" Bess asked. "He doesn't know about any of this, does he?"

"No," Marisa said. "And he has no idea why my mother broke up with him, either. But I'm sure he was upset when I started dating Devon. I know he thinks I'm terrible for Devon."

"He's wrong," Bess said firmly.

Marisa shook her head. "I'm not so sure. My life's a mess. Devon and I aren't even together." She sniffled. "I know it sounds dumb, but my birthday's tomorrow, and I just feel so— depressed."

Bess smiled. "Just wait until—"

Nancy hoped Bess wasn't about to ruin the

surprise party that Eric was throwing for Marisa. She silenced Bess with a stern look.

"Wait until what?" Marisa asked. "I hope no one's planning a surprise party. I threw a party for Eric a few months ago, and he swore he'd get even with me. You guys would tell me if he was planning to ruin my birthday with something so embarrassing, wouldn't you?"

"Of course," Bess said quickly. "I was just going to say, 'Wait until tomorrow.' I'll bet you'll have a great birthday."

Nancy cleared her throat. "Marisa. We may have one mystery solved, but we still have no idea how Eric or anyone else wound up with your grandmother's counterfeit money."

"I *do* have an idea," Marisa said.

"Really?" Nancy sat up straight. "I'm all ears."

"None of the counterfeit money resurfaced until the Guiding Eyes came to River Heights," Marisa said. "Now, Penny Rosen reads Braille, and my grandmother's papers were there for her to see, too. She could have been dipping into the supply of fake money. And she's spent a lot of time at the university, meeting with me and buying supplies for the school. Maybe that's why most of the money turned up at Westmoor."

"The hidden money we found at the inn hadn't been touched in years," Nancy said. "It was covered in dust. And Penny seemed as surprised as we were when we found it," Nancy said.

"She probably was," Marisa said. "My grandmother never mentioned the hidden room in any of the documents I read. But if Penny knew that there was money to be found, maybe she searched the inn. She's been the only sighted person there on a regular basis. If *I* found the phony twenty stuffed in a drawer, she may very well have come across more money."

"That's still a pretty big leap," Nancy said.

"I don't know," Marisa said. "I've been going over my grandmother's financial statements, and they're a mess. If my grandmother was such a whiz at the stock market, why couldn't she balance her checkbook?"

"What does that have to do with Penny?" Bess asked.

"I think Penny altered my grandmother's checkbook to make it seem as if she had less money than she really did. Then she pocketed the difference."

Marisa bit her lip. "I know it sounds like a wild accusation, but I have a bad feeling about Penny. She seems too anxious to give up on the school in River Heights." Marisa drummed her fingers on the table. "Oh, I don't know. Does anyone have any other ideas?"

"Not tonight. I'm too tired." Bess yawned. "Come on, Casey. It's time for bed."

George stood. "I'd better get going, too. I was

up at the crack of dawn this morning. See you all tomorrow." She walked with Bess to take Casey out.

Marisa stood up. "I'm exhausted, too. Good night, Nancy."

"Good night," Nancy said wearily.

Nancy wanted nothing more than to go home and sleep in her own cozy bed. Still, she didn't feel comfortable leaving Bess alone with Marisa. She wanted to believe Marisa's and Devon's stories. She truly liked both of them. But she also knew she had no proof that either of them was telling the truth.

Nancy heard the door open when Bess returned with Casey. "Bess? Do you mind if I spend the night, too?"

"You still don't trust Marisa, do you?" Bess spoke quietly.

Nancy shook her head. "I wish I did, but I'm not sure."

"I'm sure," Bess said. "But if it will make you feel better, by all means—stay." She smiled. "You can cook us breakfast in the morning. Something special for Marisa's birthday. Speaking of which—Café Olé has reopened, so Marisa's party is on for tomorrow night. Eric told me when I went to get Marisa today. You're in charge of getting her there on time. Okay?"

"Will do," Nancy said with a yawn. Tomorrow

sounded like a long day. Right now all she wanted was a good night's sleep. She hoped Casey would sleep through the night.

As it turned out, Casey slept soundly, but Nancy did not. She tossed and turned on the sofa bed in the den, which creaked every time she moved.

During one of her wakeful periods, she came up with a plan. First thing in the morning, she would go to the library and borrow a book on Braille. If she could look at Emmaline's papers and decipher them herself, then she would be satisfied, she decided. She would know whether Marisa was telling the truth.

In the morning Nancy fed and watered the dogs. She then set the table, poured three glasses of orange juice, and cooked blueberry pancakes, bacon, and scrambled eggs for three.

Marisa yawned as she sat down at the table. Nancy set a plate in front of her. "Happy birthday," she said in as cheery a voice as she could muster.

Marisa smiled. "Thanks." She reached out and touched the warm plate. "Uh . . . I hope you didn't go to a lot of trouble, Nancy. It's nothing personal, but I can't stand the thought of food before nine o'clock in the morning."

"Oh," Nancy said. "No. After all, it's your birthday."

Marisa sipped some orange juice. "This should hold me till lunch."

Bess stood up and took a box of cornflakes from the cupboard.

Nancy's eyes widened. "This isn't enough food for you? You're having cereal, too?"

"I'm having only cereal," Bess said apologetically. "I weighed myself this morning. I've been eating too many cookies. I need to go on a diet."

Nancy poured syrup over her stack of pancakes. "So what should I do with all this food?"

"I'll take it to George," Bess said. "She's loading up on carbohydrates before her next race."

"Good," Nancy said. She finished her pancakes, then quickly did the dishes before taking Marisa to school.

After she dropped off Marisa, Nancy headed home to pick up the book she had borrowed on counterfeiting. Then she drove to the central library, where she returned the book along with Bess's copy of *Raising a Well-Adjusted Puppy*.

In the nonfiction section, Nancy found the book Bess had requested on dog-obedience training. She also found five books about blindness. None of them, however, had a copy of the Braille alphabet. Nancy went up to one of the librarians and explained what she was looking for. "We've had many requests for books on blindness and guide dogs since Emmaline Whitby's bequest to the Guiding Eyes." The librarian smiled. "Mrs. Whitby would be ecstatic. She was a great benefactor of our library. We miss her."

The librarian took off her reading glasses. "Unfortunately, the library owns only one book with a copy of the Braille alphabet. I happen to know this because another person requested the same information a few weeks ago, and he checked out the book. I can find out when it's due, if you'd like."

"Thanks," Nancy said. "That would be helpful."

The librarian typed some information into the computer. "Hmm . . ." she said. "The young man who checked it out is one of our library volunteers. I believe Eric's due to work this afternoon. Maybe he'll return the book then."

"Eric Pavlik?" Nancy asked.

The librarian nodded. "Do you know him?"

"Yes," Nancy said. "He seems to be a dedicated volunteer."

"Oh, yes," the librarian said. "A hard worker, and very intelligent. Because of his volunteer work with the visually impaired, he wants to learn everything he can about the Guiding Eyes." The librarian pulled a reference book from a shelf behind her. "If you'd like, I can give you the telephone number of the Braille Institute. I'm sure they could provide you with the information you need."

Nancy copied down the phone number. She thanked the librarian for her help and walked to the front desk to check out Bess's book. As she passed through the periodicals section, she decided to try looking up Marisa's parents' obituaries. After all, Nancy thought, she still had only Marisa's word that Susan Whitby had died.

Nancy sat down at the microfiche reader and skimmed through pages of obituaries from the Milwaukee newspaper. Without too much trouble, she found a notice that Raymond and Susan Whitby Henares had been killed in a car accident a little less than two years earlier. According to the paper, they were survived by one daughter, Marisa, and Raymond's mother, Luz, who lived in the Philippines. There was no mention of Emmaline Whitby.

Nancy looked at the picture of Marisa's parents. They were young, smiling, happy. They looked as if they didn't have a care in the world.

Nancy turned off the microfiche reader. A tight, sad feeling settled in the pit of her stomach. Marisa had lost her parents and her grandmother. She had lost her sight. This week her dog had been taken, her life had been threatened, and she had broken up with her boyfriend. Now Nancy suspected her of a major crime. Nancy sighed. She hoped she was wrong. She wanted to believe Marisa. But if Marisa was innocent—who was guilty?

Why did the old counterfeit money suddenly resurface? Who vandalized the inn? And who threatened Marisa? These questions ran through Nancy's head as she drove back to Bess's house. If Emmaline was the counterfeiter, she didn't work alone. Frank Goetz and Don Blevins might have been her accomplices, but were there others? And could other members of the old counterfeiting ring be involved in the recent incidents? If so, they had eluded the police for twenty-five years. How would Nancy track them down now?

Nancy arrived at the Marvin house and jumped out of the car with Bess's library book. "Bess!" Nancy called as she entered the foyer. Mrs. Marvin's potted palm tree lay on its side. Nancy bent to turn it upright and Casey ran to greet her. "What did you do now, Casey?" Nancy rubbed the puppy's head affectionately. Casey followed Nancy into the living room. Books, papers, and slightly chewed laundry covered the floor. Bess sat on the sofa, her head buried in her hands. Nancy drew in a deep breath. "I think I brought that dog-obedience book just in time."

Bess looked up. Her eyes were red. "It's not Casey's fault. She had a very nerve-racking morning," she said. "We were robbed."

124

13

Birthday Surprise

"Robbed?" Nancy repeated. She sat down next to Bess. "Did you call the police?"

Bess shook her head. "No. I wanted to ask you first." She gestured around the room. "I think this might have something to do with the counterfeiting case."

"Why?" Nancy asked.

"The only thing that was taken was Mrs. Whitby's sewing machine," Bess said. "Who knows why, but I'm sure it's not a coincidence. But why would anybody want that one piece? Marisa said it wasn't particularly valuable."

"I don't know," Nancy said. "Are you sure nothing else was stolen?"

Bess nodded. "I'm sure. But my parents aren't going to be too happy about the broken window in the laundry room—that's how the thief got in." Bess shook her head. "I was gone for twenty minutes. I was taking your breakfast to George."

Nancy bent down and picked up a handkerchief from the scattered laundry on the floor. She used it to lift the telephone receiver. "I'm definitely calling the police. They can send someone to dust for fingerprints."

Nancy phoned Detective Lee, who promised to have uniformed officers at the Marvins' house within the hour.

As Nancy hung up the phone, the doorbell rang. Bess ushered Marisa and Misty into the living room.

"How did you get here?" Bess asked Marisa.

Marisa flushed. "Devon gave me a ride."

Bess grinned. "Well, that's one good thing that's happened today."

Marisa sighed. "Yeah. I think so. We had a good talk." She made her way to the couch and sat down. "Bess, what am I stepping on? Is it laundry?"

"Yes. I would pick it up," Bess explained, "but this is officially a crime scene."

Marisa groaned. "What happened?"

"I'm sorry to say that someone stole your grandmother's sewing machine," Bess said.

"*Your* sewing machine, you mean," Marisa said. "That's terrible. What else was taken?"

"Nothing," Bess replied.

126

"Nothing?" Marisa frowned. "This has something to do with the counterfeit money, doesn't it?"

"We think so," Nancy said.

"I can't believe this. Did you call the police?" Marisa asked.

"Yes," Bess said. "And you don't want to hang around here while the police poke around the house. It's your birthday. Nancy, why don't you do something with Marisa?"

"Good idea," Nancy said. She knew it was her job to keep Marisa occupied until her surprise party that evening at Café Olé. "Do you think you could teach me Braille, Marisa?"

Bess looked shocked. "That's not exactly what I had in mind for birthday entertainment."

Marisa laughed. "That's okay. I'd love to do something useful. Why do you want to learn Braille?"

"So I can read your grandmother's journal—some of it, at least," Nancy said.

"And check out my story, I suppose," Marisa said. "Very sensible. That's what I would do if I were you."

"Is that okay with you?" Nancy asked.

"Absolutely," Marisa said.

"I tried to get a book on Braille at the library," Nancy explained, "but Eric had already checked it out."

Marisa smiled. "Eric's amazing. He's always

wanted to learn Braille. I'm sure he's the best volunteer the library's ever had—and they've had many."

"Wait a minute." Nancy snapped her fingers. "The librarian told me today that your grandmother was a major benefactor of the library."

Marisa nodded. "I didn't know that, but I'm not surprised. She loved to read."

"Then I'd bet she took advantage of their volunteer reader service," Nancy said.

"I'm sure she must have," Marisa agreed. "I never thought about it before."

"If your grandmother used a reader, that person would have had access to her house, too," Nancy said. "Not that the volunteer was necessarily involved in the counterfeiting ring, but maybe he or she could tell us a little more about your grandmother's personal life."

"That's a great idea," Marisa said. "Eric and I got to know each other through his volunteer work. If my grandmother had the same volunteer for a number of years, she may have developed a relationship with that person." Marisa stood. "I know the volunteer coordinator at the library. Why don't I call him?"

Nancy handed Marisa the handkerchief so she could make the call without smudging any fingerprints the intruder might have left on the telephone. Marisa dialed the number and asked to speak with Leo Malone. They chatted for a moment. Finally, she said, "I was calling to see if my grandmother, Emmaline Whitby, used a volunteer reader." Marisa twirled her hair around her finger. "She did? Could you tell me the reader's name?" Marisa drew in a deep breath. "Oh. Yes, that's all I need to know. Thanks, Leo. 'Bye."

Marisa hung up the phone. She turned to Nancy and Bess. Her face was pale. "My grandmother's volunteer reader for the past three years was Eric."

"Why do you look so upset?" Bess asked. "Eric's a nice guy. Why should we be surprised that he volunteered for your grandmother? That doesn't mean he's involved with the counterfeiting."

"No," Marisa said, "but why didn't he tell me?"

"Some people are like that," Bess said. "You know, silently doing good deeds—not drawing attention to themselves."

"I think what Marisa means," Nancy said, "is that Eric worked at the inn. He was caught spending counterfeit money. Later thousands of dollars' worth of counterfeit money was found at the inn. Was Eric trying to hide something when he decided not to mention his connection to Candlelight Inn?"

129

"Maybe he figured out that my grandmother was the counterfeiter," Marisa said. "Maybe he was trying to protect her, as I was."

"Maybe," Nancy said. "But if Eric's actually involved in these incidents, I don't think you should spend time alone with him until we investigate further, Marisa."

"Agreed." Marisa massaged Misty's ears. "I didn't expect a happy birthday, but I didn't think it would be this depressing." She adjusted Misty's harness. "Do you mind if we go to the inn?" she asked Nancy. "I'd love to teach you some Braille. Then we could both skim through my grandmother's papers for any mention of Eric's name. Besides, I told Penny I'd stop by if I had time."

Nancy glanced at her watch. It was almost three o'clock. Three more hours until Marisa's party. "Sure. That's a good idea. And I don't have any plans until this evening."

Nancy parked her car along the deserted driveway at Candlelight Inn. An apple fell from an ancient tree onto the hood. "Penny's car isn't here," Nancy told Marisa.

Marisa opened the car door for Misty. "I know. She had some Guiding Eyes business in Chicago. She'll be back tomorrow. And she'll be thrilled if I get some paperwork out of the way before then."

Nancy raised her collar as a gust of wind whistled through the trees and seemed to blow right through her. Marisa unlocked the front door. Nancy entered the foyer first. She flipped the light switch, but nothing happened.

"Did you pay the electric bill?" Nancy asked Marisa.

"Yes," Marisa said. "The bulb burned out yesterday, and—" She paused. "Did you hear something?"

"No. But I'm sure your sense of hearing is better developed than mine."

"This old house makes a lot of noises," Marisa said as she began to walk down the hall. "It's pretty creepy sometimes."

Misty let out a low growl that was so ferocious, a shiver ran up Nancy's spine.

"What is it, Misty?" Marisa stopped walking.

Nancy blinked as the living room lights flickered on.

Eric entered the foyer from the living room. "Surprise!" he shouted.

"Oh, no. A birthday party." Marisa laughed. "I can't believe you did this, Eric. You know I hate surprises."

"So do I," Nancy murmured. She locked eyes with Eric. He had a gun, and it was trained on Nancy.

14

Do or Die

"Is anyone else here?" Marisa asked, entering the living room. "My voice is echoing . . ."

Nancy took a step backward and Eric cocked his gun. "Don't move," he commanded.

Marisa gasped. "Is that a gun?"

"Yes," Nancy replied tersely.

"Oh, no." Marisa hung her head. "Eric, what have you done?"

"I was at the library this afternoon and talked to Leo Malone. I heard you were asking questions about me, Marisa." Eric kept the gun pointed at Nancy. "You put her up to it, didn't you, Nancy?"

Eric motioned for Nancy to sit on one of the high-backed chairs. Nancy paused, her mind racing. She and Marisa and Misty outnumbered

Eric. Maybe they could overpower him. But Eric had a gun. No, it would be best to cooperate with Eric, Nancy decided.

Eric stepped closer to Nancy. "I said, sit down," he ordered. Without waiting for her to move, he shoved her into the chair.

While Eric's back was turned, Marisa and Misty inched toward the door. Eric whirled on them. "Where do you think you're going?"

Marisa stopped. "Nowhere. I—" She pressed up against the table. A vase fell to the floor and shattered. For a split second, Eric looked down.

Seizing the moment, Nancy lunged for Eric's gun and grabbed it. Startled, Eric's trigger finger sent a shot through the ceiling.

A frightened Misty bolted from the room, knocking Nancy off-balance. Eric regained his composure and wrestled the gun from Nancy.

"You're lucky I don't kill you right now." Eric wiped his brow. "Get back into that chair—now!" he shouted.

Without Misty at her side, Marisa looked lost. Nancy reluctantly sat back down and let Eric tie her hands with a rope from his backpack. Then he tied her legs. Next, he led Marisa to a chair and tied her arms and legs. "I hope I'm not hurting you," he said.

"Of course you're hurting me." Marisa wiggled her bound wrists. "Why are you doing this?"

Eric looked pained. "I love you, Marisa. I thought you loved me, too."

"I care for you, Eric," Marisa said gently. "I always will."

Eric's eyes were bright. "I knew it. Devon's not right for you, Marisa. *I'm* right for you. Deep down in your heart, you know that's true. I'm not going to be an out-of-work actor like Devon. I'll be a successful architect. I'll provide for you. I'll give you everything you ever wanted."

"I already have everything I want. And I don't need anyone to provide for me," Marisa said.

Eric smiled. "I've always loved your determination. I love so many things about you. Spending these past few days with you—taking you to class, knowing where you'd be at every moment—I don't want that to end. I want to be with you forever."

Nancy shivered. Eric had been following Marisa's daily schedule. He had probably been watching them all. No wonder he had been able to get in and out of Bess's house in twenty minutes—if he was the person who had stolen the sewing machine. And if he was, why?

"I'm sorry we have to spend your birthday this way," Eric told Marisa. "I had a nice surprise planned, but Nancy ruined it."

Marisa gritted her teeth. "I don't think *Nancy* ruined it."

134

"You're right." Eric leaned back on his heels. "Your *grandmother* ruined it. Do you think I would have volunteered to help her if I'd known she was a criminal? No. And some gratitude she showed me—paying me off with counterfeit money."

"Wait a minute," Nancy said. "You just said you were volunteering. Why did you take Emmaline Whitby's money at all?"

"I was volunteering as a reader," Eric explained. "All the other stuff I did—paying her bills, sorting her mail—she paid me for that. Not very well, but she paid me."

"Then *you* were my grandmother's bookkeeper. I looked through her checkbook," Marisa said accusingly. "It's a mess, and you got A's in accounting. Why is that?"

"So maybe I was a little sloppy." Eric waved the gun in the air. "Okay, so maybe I even took a little bit of her money. What's the big deal? She had so much, she never missed it."

Eric knelt beside Marisa's chair. "I only did it for you, Marisa. Your grandmother wasn't going to give it to you. You were her only living relative. You deserved to inherit her fortune, and I wanted you to have it. She left the Guiding Eyes everything and you got nothing."

"Not nothing," Marisa corrected. "My grandmother gave me her furniture, she paid my law school tuition, and most important, I got the chance to know and love her. I would never ask anything more."

Marisa cleared her throat. "Besides, I'll need to use guide dogs for the rest of my life. My grandmother was thinking of me when she left her money to the Guiding Eyes."

"Don't be naive," Eric said. "The Guiding Eyes is looking for any excuse to get out of this project in River Heights. The organization wants to use your grandmother's money to line their own pockets. Emmaline should have pulled her little scam on them—not me."

"Scam?" Marisa squirmed uncomfortably. "What are you talking about?"

"After your grandmother realized she didn't have long to live, I was helping her put her affairs in order. She may have been sick, but she was still sharp—I'll give her that. One day, out of the blue, she gave me a whole bunch of money, thanked me, and said she didn't need my help anymore. She died a few days later—and that's when this nightmare started."

"Mrs. Whitby had found the discrepancies in her finances and realized you'd embezzled money from her," Nancy said. "So she got rid of you and paid you off in counterfeit money."

"Very good," Eric said sarcastically. "You figured it out. I myself didn't figure it out until you found the stash of counterfeit bills at the inn.

136

That's when I realized Emmaline must have given me the bad money to get back at me."

"Grandmother knew you and I were friends," Marisa said. "I can't believe she didn't warn me about you."

"I couldn't believe it, either," Eric said. "But you clearly had no idea where I got the counterfeit money. You rushed to defend me. I was glad, of course. But after Nancy got me off the hook, I needed you to stop digging for information. The closer you came to learning who the counterfeiter was, the closer you came to my secret. I knew I couldn't let you find out that I'd been stealing money from your grandmother's bank account. Of course, I did it for you—but I didn't think you'd understand."

"No," Marisa said, "I wouldn't have understood."

"That's when I remembered the letter." Eric stood up and began pacing.

Marisa frowned. "What letter?"

"Your grandmother wrote you a letter," Eric said, "for you to read after her death."

"I never got any letter," Marisa said.

"I know. I watched her hide it," Eric explained, "but she didn't know I saw her. After the phony money was found at the inn, I realized your grandmother must have found out about my creative management of her bank account. I was afraid the letter might tell you what I had done."

"So you broke into the inn and stole the letter," Nancy said.

"Wrong!" A smile spread across Eric's face. "I stumped the famous detective. Actually, I'd made myself a copy of Emmaline's key to Marisa's apartment. I let myself into Marisa's apartment and stole the letter."

"That's when you left her the threatening computer message," Nancy said. "And you also put the glass in our food at the restaurant."

Eric nodded. "I didn't want to hurt you, Marisa. I knew you'd feel the glass with your fork before you took one bite of your meal. I only wanted you to give up the counterfeiting case." He sighed. "I had no idea it would be so difficult."

"How did my grandmother's letter end up in my apartment?" Marisa asked.

"Your grandmother gave Misty a can of dog treats just before she died," Eric said.

Marisa nodded. "And?"

"She had taped the letter to the inside of the can. She knew when the can was empty, you would run your fingers along the bottom and find the letter. I suppose she figured the letter was safe there from any curious people at Candlelight Inn—like me."

Marisa smiled. "And she knew Misty averages three treats a day. I was close to the bottom of the can."

Misty slunk into the room and, shaking, pressed up against Marisa's leg.

Eric laughed. "I guess she heard the word 'treat.' I always liked you, Misty. You're a smart dog."

Misty growled and bared her teeth. "What's the matter, girl?" Eric asked Misty. "We used to be best friends."

Nancy closed her eyes. In Eric's mind, he was protecting Marisa because he was madly in love with her. The threats, the theft, the lies—he'd done it all for Marisa. Everything made sense— almost. But who had vandalized Candlelight Inn? Who had stolen Bess's sewing machine? And why?

"Wake up, Nancy." Eric tapped Nancy on the shoulder. "I've got some important work for that detective brain of yours."

Eric reached into his pocket and fished out a crumpled letter. He held it up in front of Nancy. The pages were filled with Braille dots, with the corresponding letters written underneath the Braille.

Eric smirked. "I hear I beat you to the library's only book with the Braille alphabet. Sorry. I had to work on this project. But I returned it this afternoon—it's all yours now."

Nancy squinted at Eric's wobbly translation of the Braille document. It was the second page of

Emmaline's letter to Marisa. "Where's page one?"

"Page one deals with the matter of Emmaline's checkbook and her unfounded accusations against me. I incinerated it," Eric said. "But page two is very interesting. Read it out loud. I want Marisa to hear it—after all, it is for her."

Nancy took a deep breath. " 'Marisa, you are no longer blind to my faults,' " she read. " 'You know about my past. This is not the legacy I wanted to leave you. A defective gene has passed from generation to generation in this family, causing blindness. Some were spared—you and I were not. Thankfully, you escaped a far worse affliction, which is the greed I inherited from my forefathers. Edward Taper was willing to do anything for money. So, I'm sorry to say, was I. A valuable family heirloom has been handed down from Edward. Now, Marisa, it will be yours. Do with it what you will. I know you will use it for a worthwhile purpose. And in case prying eyes read this letter, please study the remainder closely. My secretary will furnish you with the aforementioned treasure. I've hidden it in a safe place. And remember—a stitch in time saves nine. Money doesn't grow on trees. Love always, Grandmother.' "

Marisa's face was frozen.

"What do you think?" Eric asked.

"I don't know," Marisa said. "I mean, I don't understand."

"I understand one thing." Nancy turned to Eric. "You broke into the inn to look for Emmaline's treasure. 'Money doesn't grow on trees'—that's why you hacked at the oak tree outside. And Bess's sewing machine . . ."

"Right, right," Eric said. " 'A stitch in time.' " Eric took a step toward Nancy. "That's the easy part, Nancy. Unfortunately, there was no treasure in the tree, there was no treasure in the sewing machine—there was no treasure anywhere."

Eric pointed the gun at Nancy's head. "Where's the treasure, Nancy? And if you don't know—you're going to die."

15

Nancy's Legacy

Nancy took a deep breath. "May I read the letter again?" she asked Eric.

"Don't stall," Eric said. He held up the letter and let Nancy take a quick look.

" 'My secretary will furnish you with the aforementioned treasure,' " Nancy repeated. "Emmaline didn't have a secretary, did she?"

"*I* was the closest thing she had to a secretary," Eric said. "Obviously, I don't know anything about the treasure. Weren't you paying attention? If this is the best you can do—"

"As I was saying," Nancy interrupted, "Emmaline didn't have a secretary working for her. A *secretary* is also another name for a piece of furniture—a desk, like the one Emmaline has in the study."

"Which matches Bess's sewing machine,"
Marisa added. "Okay. Now we're getting somewhere." Eric kept his gun trained on Nancy and
Marisa as he backed out of the foyer. "Don't try
anything funny. I'll be right back."

As Eric's footsteps faded, Marisa pushed Misty
toward Nancy. "Hold out your hands," she whispered.

Nancy thrust her bound hands toward the dog.
Misty sank her teeth into the thick rope. Within
seconds, she had chewed all the way through.
Nancy moved her feet from underneath the
chair, and Misty went to work on the rope that
bound her ankles together.

"The desk is locked!" Eric called from the
study. "Where's the key?"

"It's at my apartment!" Marisa shouted back.
Eric stormed back into the room. Nancy quickly
hid her hands in the folds of her sweater and
stuck her feet under the chair. Misty had almost
chewed through the rope around her ankles.

"Are you lying to me?" Eric asked. "Because if
you don't have the key, I'm going to break the
lock. You don't want me to do that, do you?"

With a mighty tug, Nancy freed her ankles.
Eric looked down. "Hey!" he shouted when he
saw the loose ropes. He stepped toward Nancy,
waving the gun.

Misty let out a terrifying bark and leaped at
Eric. The gun flew from his hand. Misty pinned

him against the wall, her paws on his shoulders and her teeth inches from his throat.

Nancy scrambled to her feet. While Misty held Eric against the wall, Nancy picked up the loose ropes from the floor. They were still long enough to be used on Eric. Misty let Nancy close enough to tie the ropes first around Eric's wrists, then his ankles.

When Eric was securely tied, Nancy scooped up the gun, went into the kitchen, and called the police. Through the kitchen window, she saw a black sports car partially hidden in the bushes behind the inn. That must be Eric's car, she thought. It was the car that had nearly run her over outside Marisa's apartment.

Nancy grabbed a knife from the kitchen, then hurried into the living room and used it to cut through the ropes binding Marisa. With Misty's help, Marisa and Nancy took Eric into the study. Marisa offered Misty a treat from the can on Penny's desk. Misty refused to take it. Her eyes were fixed on Eric. If he twitched his finger, she snapped at him.

Marisa shuffled through Penny's desk and found a tiny key. "Voilà." She handed it to Nancy.

"The key to the secretary?" Nancy asked.

Marisa nodded. "Yes. I don't ordinarily lie," she told Eric, "but under the circumstances, I felt it was justified."

Nancy jiggled the key in the lock of the secretary. The glass doors covering the shelves on top of the desk rattled. Finally, the lock turned. Nancy pulled down the desktop. It became an uncluttered, flat surface for writing. Pigeonholes and drawers were at the back of the desk.

One by one, Nancy removed the drawers. Behind the bottom drawer on the right, she found a hidden compartment. She reached in and pulled out a black, leatherbound book. The title was in Braille. She handed it to Marisa.

Marisa ran her finger across the cover. " 'Family Bible,' " she read.

" 'A stitch in time saves nine,' " Nancy repeated. " 'Money doesn't grow on trees.' That's what your grandmother's note says. Does the bible have a family tree?" Nancy asked Marisa.

Marisa opened the book and ran her fingers over the thick pages. "Here we go. On page nine." Marisa's fingers stopped, and she smiled. "Here's my name. Wait a minute," she said. "What's this?"

Nancy moved over to look at the object in Marisa's hand. It was a leather pouch stitched to the binding of the bible. With trembling hands, Marisa opened it. She pulled out a bill. "Is this money? It sort of feels like it—but sort of not."

Eric craned his neck and looked. "Play money," he moaned. "I went to all this trouble for phony fifty-dollar bills. Your grandmother was really something else."

Nancy examined the bill. "This is real money—real money from 1874. I saw bills like this on display at the historical society the other day. They're valuable to collectors."

Nancy counted the bills in the pouch. "At face value, you have one thousand dollars here. I'm no expert, but it must be worth much more."

There was a knock at the door. "Police!"

Detective Lee greeted Nancy with a smile. "I understand you've solved the counterfeiting case?"

An hour later Marisa and Nancy had finished giving their statements to Detective Lee. Eric was in custody, and this time he had to find his own lawyer. Nancy and Marisa were free to leave police headquarters.

"Let's go to Café Olé," Nancy said brightly.

Marisa groaned. "You're kidding. I'm ready for bed."

"It's your birthday," Nancy said. "Come on."

"I see," Marisa said. "There really *is* a surprise party, right?"

"Promise me you'll *pretend* you're surprised," Nancy said. "Otherwise, Bess will kill me."

Marisa laughed. "I think it's the least I can do—after all you've done for me."

* * *

One week later Bess and Nancy sat with Bess's parents at the Marvins' dining room table. "It's lonely without Casey here." Bess speared a section of grapefruit.

"I miss her, too," Mr. Marvin said. "But my sinuses don't."

Mr. Marvin's cold had miraculously disappeared while he and Mrs. Marvin were vacationing in Florida. But when they returned home, the cold came back more ferociously than before. The doctor diagnosed an intense allergy to dogs, and there was only one cure. Bess had to find Casey a new home. Luckily, the Marshalls had agreed to adopt Casey. Amber had done such a good job of helping to care for the puppy at the Marvins' that her parents decided she was responsible enough to raise her for the next fifteen months.

"At least I can visit Casey whenever I want," Bess said. "She's growing so fast."

The doorbell rang. Bess opened the door to Amber, Devon, and Marisa. "Where's Misty?" Bess asked.

"We left her at our house because of your father's allergies," Devon explained.

"Oh, you're eating," Marisa said. "I can hear the silverware clinking. We should have called first."

"That's okay," Bess said. "Come on in."

Devon led Marisa into the dining room. When

they sat down, Bess passed around a plate of Hannah's lemon poppyseed muffins, which Nancy had brought over.

"We just took Casey to her first class at obedience school," Amber said.

Devon took a muffin. "We thought you'd like a progress report."

"She learned to sit and heel," Amber said. "Well, sort of. But she was definitely the best one in the class."

"I understand there wouldn't be a class if it weren't for Marisa's generous donation to the Guiding Eyes," Mrs. Marvin said. "They came very close to having to give up the project in River Heights."

Marisa blushed. "It's no big deal. My grandmother wanted me to use the family money for a good cause. Anyhow, I kept half of it," she said. "And half of eighty thousand dollars is still a lot of money."

"Enough to rebuild the Marshall family business," Devon said. "Marisa didn't keep the money for herself. She lent it to my father."

"He'll pay me back, of course," Marisa said. "We have a written agreement," she added. "After all, I *am* a law student."

"The Guiding Eyes is naming the school's new library for Marisa," Devon said proudly.

"None of this would have been possible without Nancy," Marisa pointed out.

"The breeder brought eight new puppies to the school this morning. Nancy, guess what Penny named one of them?" Amber fidgeted with excitement.

Nancy laughed. "I have no idea."

"There was one particularly inquisitive golden retriever—a beautiful redhead, I understand." Marisa smiled. "Her name is Nancy Drew."

Masquerade as Nancy Drew
to catch a thief in
The Phantom of Venice!

Il Fantasma — the Phantom — is stealing Venice's most valuable treasures! Witnesses say he wears a mask as his disguise, but it's *Carnevale* and everyone dresses in elaborate costumes to celebrate. There's no way to tell if a masked person is the thief or a reveler!

You, as Nancy Drew, must take the case and infiltrate a crime ring to catch the phantom thief before he strikes again!

dare to play

PC CD   PC

PC
Adventure
Game #18

NANCY DREW
The Phantom of Venice

For Mystery Fans 10 to Adult
Order online at www.HerInteractive.com
or call 1-800-461-8787. Also in stores!
Compatible with WINDOWS® XP/Vista

EVERYONE
E
Mild Violence
ESRB CONTENT RATING   www.esrb.org

Copyright © 2008 Her Interactive, Inc. HER INTERACTIVE, the HER INTERACTIVE logo and DARE TO PLAY are trademarks of Her Interactive, Inc. NANCY DREW is a trademark of Simon & Schuster, Inc. Licensed by permission of Simon & Schuster, Inc.

CAROLYN KEENE
NANCY DREW
GIRL DETECTIVE

Secret Sabotage

Serial Sabotage

Sabotage Surrender

Secret Identity

Identity Theft

Identity Revealed

Model Crime

Model Menace

Model Suspect

INVESTIGATE THESE THREE THRILLING MYSTERY TRILOGIES!

Available wherever books are sold!

Aladdin • Simon & Schuster Children's Publishing • KIDS.SimonandSchuster.com

FRANKLIN W. DIXON

THE HARDY BOYS

Undercover Brothers®

INVESTIGATE THESE TWO ADVENTUROUS MYSTERY TRILOGIES WITH AGENTS FRANK AND JOE HARDY!

#28 Galaxy X

#29 X-plosion!

#31 Killer Mission

#32 Private Killer

#30 The X-Factor

#33 Killer Connections

From Aladdin
Published by Simon & Schuster